HUNTED

BY

MONIQUE DR GLIOZZI

Tellwell Talent
www.tellwell.ca

ISBN
978-0-2288-1784-0 (Hardcover)
978-0-2288-1783-3 (Paperback)
978-0-2288-1785-7 (eBook)

Disclaimer

This novel's story is fictitious. Certain long-standing institutions, public offices and agencies are mentioned, but the characters involved are entirely imaginary. Any resemblance to actual persons living or deceased is entirely coincidental.

Table of Contents

Acknowledgements

I would like to express my gratitude to the following people who have helped me create and publish my first and second novels:

Alexandra Davies, my editor who taught me to how to keep things simple.

Tim Lindsay, CEO and founder of Tellwell Publishing.

Philip Gray, my publishing consultant and Jonveth Tabar, my project manager.

Ruth Callaghan, a dear family friend and journalist, who pointed me in the right direction early in the project. Mark and Diana Guthridge helping with the book launch and promotion, making this project a real adventure.

Finally, to all the avid readers of fiction who continue to inspire today's authors.

To my husband and extended family, always loyal, supportive and humorous.

With love.

"The real in us is silent; the acquired is talkative."

—Kahlil Gibran

Prologue

There is something majestic about the mountain range spanning across the alpine states of Austria, Lichtenstein and Slovenia. The Swiss Alps formed millions of years ago a result of the African and Eurasian tectonic plates colliding. Standing proudly with snow-covered peaks, their shadows loom over the river Rhine and its townships as if protecting them from the elements of a bitter winter.

Over the winter months, tourists enjoy skiing on the vast and challenging slopes. But not today, for it is spring in Grindelwald, the largest village in the Jungfrau region. The change of season brings a change in recreational activities for tourists and locals alike. Hiking, camping and helicopter tours of the glacial gorges would be popular over the coming months.

Chapter One

Irma Trauber opened the window of her small apartment located on the top floor of the Kirbana Hotel, which she had managed for over ten years. Standing at the window, she allowed the sun to warm her face as she enjoyed the view of the Wetterhorn and the fresh alpine air.

"Another day in this paradise," Irma thought, permitting her mind to wander in reminiscence of her youth, growing up with extended family, all employed in the hospitality business. It was on a spring day like this that she had met a shy young apprentice called Otto, working as a kitchen hand in her father's guest house. Times where different then. Only after asking her father for Irma's hand in marriage was Otto permitted to court this beautiful slender twenty-year-old with eyes as green as emeralds. Both were ambitious, investing wisely into the hotel where Otto was now head Chef and which Irma now managed.

Their two sons, now young adults, lived in Munich to attend university. Irma smiled to herself as she thought of her boys, Franz and Ludwig, and how determined they had been to break family tradition and not work in the hospitality business. Ironically, both had chosen a career pathway in business management, which Irma secretly hoped would eventually bring them back to run the family hotel.

As a seasoned manager, Irma knew what awaited her downstairs. A group of Japanese tourists and a local team of soccer players were expected. It would be busy. Taking in one last deep breath of mountain air, satisfied and serene, she turned away from the window and made her way to her office. Despite being perceptive, Irma did not anticipate that a rowdy soccer team would be the least of her problems. Something more sinister was due to descend on her sanctuary.

Chapter Two

Isabella admired her wedding band one last time before removing it in order to apply moisturizing cream to her face. Nick Hauser, her husband of a few months, had planned a romantic evening after they had both had a long and grueling week at work. The newlyweds had married in a simple ceremony on the shores of Santa Monica, which was followed by a champagne breakfast with family and close friends. Fitting the cuff links Isabella had given him as an engagement present, Nick leaned against the doorframe to their en suite and watched his wife dress.

Neither had wanted an elaborate wedding celebration, but had looked forward to a luxurious honeymoon in Hawaii. That plan was dashed due to the untimely passing of Isabella's twin brother, Marco, in a skydiving accident. The twins, originally from Mexico City, had been adopted by a childless American couple, the Ashfords, after losing their entire family in the 1985 earthquake that almost destroyed the city. Both had led a life of privilege with their loving adoptive parents, following high profile careers, Isabella as chief detective of cold cases and Marco as a corporate attorney.

Nick had met his wife two years earlier when they worked together as junior detectives. Recently he had been promoted to the Special Victims Unit, which took him along a different career path to Isabella. Now, with Marco gone forever, Isabella was the only survivor of the original Fernandez family. She hoped that one day she would have a family of her own and vowed to name their children after her parents.

Lost in thought, she did not hear Nick approach her. He tapped her shoulder. Startled, she looked up at him He was concealing something behind his back.

"What?" she enquired. She straightened her posture, curious about her husband's secretive demeanor.

Without a sound, he handed her a manila envelope and waited for a reaction. Isabella took it and, while still watching her husband, opened it. She pulled out airline tickets and an itinerary for a brief holiday in Portugal.

"A belated honeymoon," Nick said, taking her into his arm and kissing her gently on the lips before she could protest.

"Nick, this is a wonderful surprise, but I still have a case to solve. You know that the longer a fugitive is allowed to be on the run, the harder it is to track him down." The fugitive was Peter Steil, wanted for triple homicide and now on the run.

Nick smiled reassuringly, promising that he would not keep her too long from her mission.

"Alright, darling," she acquiesced, feeling excited at the prospect of exploring a new country. They hugged, but Peter Steil was still very much at the forefront of the young detective's mind.

Chapter Three

Peter Steil relaxed by a small fireplace of the small cabin he was renting from a local hunter in Grindelwald. Sipping a Scotch on the rocks, he congratulated himself on the changes he had carefully planned and carried out over the better part of a year.

It had been almost eight months since he had left Los Angeles, where he was wanted for murder. A triple homicide to be exact, but now Peter was a man with a new identity. He had killed his wealthy parents for financial gain, framing his identical twin brother Patrick for the murders. It had almost been the perfect crime until Patrick, claiming his innocence and at the insistence of his attorney, had chosen to go to trial.

Being identical twins it would have been easy to frame his brother, who throughout their lives had always been easily manipulated. To the outside world the twins were considered polite, mild-mannered and sociable, which made their parents proud. Patrick had always believed Peter to be superior, after all he was older by a few minutes—he was a brother to look up to and be

6

guided by in times of trouble. Peter, on the other hand, resented his twin's hideous compulsion to be truthful, but on some level still felt the need to protect him against the schoolyard bully.

Upon reflection, perhaps confronting the bully had been a means to express his inner streak of violence, which had eventually resulted in him being expelled. His parents had sent him to military school to be reformed, which later led to Peter enlisting in the US Marine Corps, while Patrick remained at home to be spoiled by their parents. Over time, the rift between Peter and his family had grown irreparable.

When Patrick had elected to go to trial, Peter had no choice but to silence him while he was out on bail. He had made it look like a suicide. The mental image of his brother suspended from the staircase railing flashed into focus, only to be consciously dismissed by Peter. He took another sip of the chilled golden liquid from his tumbler.

Peter was sure that he had covered his tracks since leaving LA, and he was confident he would not be considered a potential suspect. But he still felt the need to be cautious. Having intentionally deserted his unit while fighting in Afghanistan and secretly returning to the US to take care of this 'family business', he was sure that the US marines had considered him missing in action—MIA—and possibly dead.

He had planned the murders for a year, and not even his buddy, Luke, with whom he had fought alongside in Iraq, had known of his deployment to Afghanistan or his MIA status. Peter stood and moved to the cabinet to help himself to another Scotch. Leaning against the window seal, he marveled at the lush vegetation that kept his cabin secluded. Exactly as he wanted it to be.

Once again allowing his proud mind to be flooded with memories, he thought back to the ride on his Kawasaki across the border into Mexico, where he had boarded a commercial flight to Milan, Italy—the capital of fashion and a beautiful city. There he enrolled in a linguistics school to perfect the Italian he had learned on his own using a Lonely Planet book and CD. It was here he befriended Giulio Del Toro, his teacher and a man of many talents with many useful connections. One such contact was a forger of documents, who for the right price could help create a new identity. Peter Steil became Peter Claasen, a helicopter pilot from Bornio.

The rest was easy. Peter moved to Bern, Switzerland, where he lodged at a small bed and breakfast, learned Swiss German for a few weeks, and then relocated to Grindelwald. It only demanded one overnight stay at the Kirbana Hotel and light-hearted conversation with Irma, the manager, before she made some recommendations that found him his lodgings and work as a helicopter guide for the local tourist bureau.

Peter felt free as a bird, almost invincible. It never once occurred to him that birds could be forced out of their well-hidden nests.

Chapter Four

Portugal was a great holiday destination, the senior travel agent in LA had told Nick. A country on the Iberian Peninsula, its west facing the Atlantic Ocean and east bordering Spain. The architecture dated back to the 1500s when Portugal had been a maritime empire. Nick had reserved a suite at the Baia Grande Hotel located on the Algarve beaches. Isabella had been taking photos of the serene coastline when Nick approached her and handed her a mimosa.

"It's only a hop, skip and jump to Spain and then across to the rest of Europe," she remarked.

"Are you thinking of extending our honeymoon, my love, or is something else on your mind?" he asked, knowing that she had been having vivid dreams again, a sign of her higher intuition.

"I keep having the same dream of a key attached to the collar of a large hawk, flying off deep into a forest at the foot of a mountain," she said, facing her husband who was studying her closely. They sat down on the sand, both facing the ocean, watching and listening to the waves crashing ashore. A small fishing boat was being unloaded by two young boys and a man who was likely to be their father. Sensing that they were being watched, the man turned to the couple and waved. Isabella and Nick returned the greeting with the same gesture.

Finishing their drinks, they returned to their suite to get ready for a guided tour into the countryside. Isabella was excited by the idea of being driven in a Jeep into the surrounding hills, but still could not shake the nagging feeling of her dream. Isabella's dreams had always been symbolic of a stressful reality. Peter Steil, the fugitive, was now a part of this reality and would haunt her until she found him.

Chapter Five

Peter was comfortable at the controls of the six-seater helicopter, returning from a guided tour of the Wetterhorn. His passengers had been enthusiastic, asking questions and taking photos with the latest technology iPhone.

Having accurately completed a weight and balance as per aviation protocol to ensure the aircraft had a safe center of gravity throughout the flight, he had the pleasure of seating a robust man in his forties in the copilot seat. The man was of few words, which Peter liked, compared to some of his colleagues who preferred idle banter. As they approached the helipad, Peter gently slowed to a landing speed, allowing the chopper to steady itself in a hover configuration, before gently touching down. The passengers applauded and alighted from the aircraft still giddy with excitement.

While securing the helicopter post-flight in line with standard procedure, Peter's mind returned to a brief trip he had planned for the following day to meet his teacher and friend, Giulio, in Milan. He was looking forward to seeing him again and attending a fashion show attended by the VIPs of society. Furthermore he hoped to see the twin models again, Sacha and her brother Toni Rafael, after sharing a wild night with them at a designer's post-event party last Christmas. Giulio and Sacha had been high school sweethearts, but drifted apart once her modeling career took off. They had remained friends and were comfortable with the arrangement, despite Toni's attempts to reunite them.

Peter drove up to his cabin, stopped short of its porch, killed the ignition and took a moment to glance around before unlocking the door and moving inside. It was a routine that had become a habit since leaving the US, which he was not inclined to change. A drill sergeant had once told him that a good soldier never changed pattern of behavior—"That way you won't miss anything when looking for the enemy," he had said. Peter made himself spaghetti with a light tomato sauce, garnished with asparagus, and ate in silence. After dinner he packed a small duffel bag with belongings to last a few days and settled in front of the television to watch the news. Satisfied that there was still no mention of him being on a 'wanted' list, he retired to bed, looking forward to being flown to Italy by a fellow pilot in a private jet.

Chapter Six

The Californian style bungalow stood at the end of a cul-de-sac shaded by trees of a quiet street in West Hollywood. Nick and Isabella had bought the property prior to getting married, keeping their respective bachelor pads as investments. Isabella completed the short walk down the driveway to collect the mail from the letter box and waved to the neighbor across the street. Before returning into the house, she paused, feeling a wave of lightheadedness and nausea. It had been three weeks since returning from Portugal and she worried she might have contracted a stomach virus that would not subside. Regaining composure she managed to return into the large kitchen where she made herself a chamomile tea. Nick had gone fishing for the weekend with a college buddy, so she was left on her own, which under different circumstances, she would have cherished. He had offered to stay home, but at her insistence had not changed his plans.

A knock at the door startled her. Through the window she could see Lorraine, a longtime friend who had offered to help her that morning with the spring cleaning. Lorraine still owned the little antique shop in Santa Monica and had herself recently married at a small chapel in Las Vegas. Her husband, Robert, was the manager of a pet store. One day, while walking his Jack Russell, Cody, along the beach where Lorraine was collecting shells, the dog escaped from his harness and ran, making a beeline for Lorraine. Cody was drawn to her instinctively. When Robert caught up with them, instead of reprimanding the dog, he was smitten by the beautiful Bohemian lady standing in front of him, and chose to ask her out to brunch. She accepted without hesitation. Not long after that encounter, they were married.

"Hi, Lorraine. Welcome to the old married folks club!" Isabella teased, hugging her friend and inviting her into the kitchen. "You look absolutely gorgeous," she remarked, offering her visitor a cup of organic tea.

"Thanks, sweetheart," her friend said, happily accepting the compliment, but noticing Isabella's pale complexion she asked, "How is that stomach bug?"

"Still there. I suppose the Mediterranean bugs are more virulent than I thought," Isabella remarked, before saying, "Lorraine, I have wanted to talk to you about something." Her good friend and confidant of several years nodded, waiting for Isabella to continue. "After so many years, I feel like my gift is failing me. I've just not had the same level of intuition regarding the cases I'm working on. It worries me that I may not be able to assist effectively in capturing Peter Steil."

Isabella looked tired and full of self-doubt, which was uncharacteristic. Lorraine gently placed her hand on that of her friend's in a gesture of complete understanding and empathy.

"Isa, sometimes the gift that we have changes in intensity through no fault of our own. There are a variety of possible explanations."

"Such as?" Isabella asked, curious.

Lorraine seized the opportunity and removed a small packet from her bag. She slid it across the table toward Isabella.

"What's this?" she asked, eyeing the packet.

"I thought that maybe you're carrying something other than a bug," she retorted, signaling inverted commas with her fingers upon uttering "a bug".

A home pregnancy test. Isabella looked at her friend, who, despite not having children of her own, had a sixth sense for a lot of things. Early stages of pregnancy included.

Isabella motioned her friend to stay in the kitchen as she took the packet and locked the guest bathroom door, where she remained for what seemed like an eternity. Lorraine moved closer to the bathroom and crouched outside the door, but it was quiet. Eventually Isabella emerged.

"It looks like Nick and I are destined to be parents," Isabella announced. The women hugged, laughed and cried. All emotions rolled into one. Isabella was relieved that she did not have terminal amoebic dysentery or something similar. She would tell her husband the news when he returned on Sunday night. Isabella was excited. Everything else at that moment was insignificant. Including the fugitive.

Chapter Seven

Milano, Italy, International Fashion Week

The models in turn made their way down the catwalk with just enough attitude to make the waiting spectators envious of their position in the world. The music had a punchy bass, adding emphasis to the artistic mood in the rented hall of the opera house, La Scala. Organizers stood in the wings, anxious that the event would run like clockwork. It did. Nobody, with exception of the models and designers, knew of the last minute glitches unfolding behind the scenes; every model came out with a calm air, displaying couture for the critics to either marvel at or criticize. Peter and Giulio sat in the front row alongside some of the world's most prominent designers.

"There she is," Giulio stated excitedly as Sacha sashayed down the runway in a black satin evening gown. Posing at the end of the catwalk, she turned her head just enough to the side to make flirtatious eye contact with Peter. Then she turned to walk back whence she had come.

"I think she remembers you," Giulio said, nudging Peter playfully. Peter smiled but had no intention of entering a romantic relationship with anybody. Unlike his twin, Peter believed people were meant to serve a purpose. "No point getting close if one is going to discard them," he would tell his naïve, romantic brother.

The show had been a success. Toni and Sacha invited the two men to the after party held at a private villa on the outskirts of Milan. The luxurious residence belonged to the daughter of Count Safini, an old aristocrat from the lineage of the last king of Italy.

The young countess, Lana Safini, was the only unmarried daughter of the family, fueling speculation among others in her social circle. The truth was that Lana was a hopeless romantic. Her choice in men had been disastrous.

The villa was swarming with security making regimented rounds of the large grounds every half hour. Santo was a well-built man and part of the armed forces, but due to the economic climate had found additional employment as private security. He looked handsome in a navy blue suit, and professional with a microscopic earpiece positioned behind his left ear. Santo diligently held his assigned position in the hall, keeping a close eye on the main entrance.

Giulio and his fashionable friends paused a moment before being granted access to the party. Santo noticed something about the young foreign man standing next to the young lady in their company. He concluded that the girl was certainly a model by her appearance and theatrics, and that the foreigner was American but spoke Italian almost without accent. His eyes met those of the stranger. Santo looked at his invitation, noticing the name: Peter

Claasen. Santo had a bad gut feeling about this guest. As a child his mother had taught him to listen to his instincts.

"Listen to your gut," she would say. "It's there for a reason, not only to digest a plate of homemade pasta." Santo decided to follow his mother's advice.

Chapter Eight

The foursome maneuvered around the ballroom, smiling and nodding at other guests, until they found Lana. The young countess was entertaining her guests with a story of her first snowboarding lesson in Saint Moritz. Peter was amused by her gesticulations and gyrations in an attempt to convey her experience, which would have been amusing to anyone who had actually witnessed it.

His mind was abruptly returned to the present when he heard his name, as Toni introduced him to Lana. Gallantly, Peter took her hand and kissed it. Lana giggled and proceeded to introduce the group to her other guests. Throughout the evening, Peter and the young countess discussed fashion and political events, both past and present. She was well-read, which surprised him, and of course he had done his homework in fashion and Italian history. Peter was by now well-versed in giving a fictional account based on his new identity.

Lana was taken by his cordial demeanor and display of etiquette. As the night went on, Lana mingled with other guests, but always found herself drawn back to Peter side. Sacha was unimpressed.

"She seems so desperate," she told her brother. "Look at her. She is all over him like a bad rash".

"He is just being polite," Toni replied, trying to reassure her and keenly aware that if she pursued Peter she would be in for a fall that he and Giulio would have to break.

Disenchanted, Sacha asked for directions to the ladies room. Standing in front of the mirror, she contemplated her next move. She removed a small compact from her purse, placed two lines of cocaine on its small mirror and snorted them with a hundred dollar bill that Peter had given her as a souvenir at their last encounter.

"There," she thought, as the almost instantaneous rush of euphoria traveled through every fiber of her slim body.

Santo had noticed the model's edginess thus had decided to follow her and wait outside the bathroom. He positioned himself in such a way that she would bump into him once she emerged. His plan worked.

"*Mi scusi, Signorina*," he said as sincerely as he could muster, catching her in his muscular arms.

Sacha held onto him, perhaps a bit longer than he had anticipated, before letting go.

"*Di niente*," she replied, smiling. Santo took the opportunity to engage her in light conversation, hoping to learn more about the American.

"You seem upset," he started. "Anything I can help you with?" he continued, demonstrating a fair command of English despite the strong Mediterranean accent.

"No. I just always fall for the wrong guys," she answered, motioning with her head in the direction of Peter.

"Why is he wrong? He seems nice to me," Santo probed.

"He is a pilot, and they have a girl at every corner of the globe," she whined.

"He is American, yes?"

Sacha nodded before adding, "Yeah, but he lives in Switzerland. Flies helicopters or something." She composed herself and thanked Santo for his concern.

"*Buona fortuna*," he called out as she walked back to the party. Sacha turned her head slightly and blew him a kiss.

Santo had enough information. Now he had to think of how to utilize it. He would obtain the security footage and study it after the party.

Chapter Nine

Peter and Lana danced the waltz, foxtrot and tango, enjoying each other's company.

Toni had met an old friend from designer school and was busy making plans for the next season of fashion, while Giulio introduced Sacha to a number of eligible men of means, distracting her from the scene unfolding on the dance floor.

In heels, Lana stood at five foot five, her dark brown hair flowing freely over her shoulders, her hazel colored eyes gazing romantically at Peter. He had an athletic build, tussled dark blond hair that he could dye brown to match his trimmed beard as part of his new persona. At times he wore colored contact lenses, but to appeal to a more sophisticated milieu, such as tonight, he sported thin, gold-rimmed spectacles. He always wore Giorgio Armani Acqua di Gio aftershave, preferring its fresh, slightly citrusy scent.

"Stay with me tonight, Peter," Lana requested as they moved from center stage toward the bar.

Handing her a flute of champagne and raising it to toast her, he spotted Sacha glaring at him from across the room. Leaning in to kiss Lana on the cheek, he whispered an acceptance to her invitation. Peter was sure that Sacha would be off his back, enabling him to indulge and feed his narcissism. After all, Lana was a true asset.

The party was winding down and guests were leaving, some in a merrier state than when they had arrived.

Peter had informed Giulio about his change of plans. The men agreed to meet back at Giulio's apartment the following day, before Peter's return to Switzerland. Sacha and Toni were nowhere in sight. Frankly, Peter didn't care.

Santo walked into the control room containing all the security monitors. His colleagues, Danilo and Patrizio, sat facing the screens and greeted him as he pulled up a chair next to them.

"Patrizio, I want you to return to the early part of the evening, say around 9:00 p.m."

"Any particular section?" he asked Santo.

"The entrance hall where the guests arrive," he requested.

Patrizio obliged, freezing and enhancing the frame when instructed. On the monitor he had a clear picture of the American. Pulling out a thumb drive from his pocket, and handing it to his colleague, he asked for this particular image and others to be stored. Danilo and Patrizio stared at Santo awaiting an explanation that never came. In truth, Santo was concerned for the safety of the young and naïve countess. Recently, he had overheard a man at the local newspaper stand discuss a brutal murder in the South of Italy. The authorities had no leads and were relying on locals to assist.

"For all we know the killer could be anywhere, even here!" the man had commented, half joking. This comment had left Santo wondering how society had become so immune to serious offenses. Now he was troubled, and after tonight felt it was his job to be curious about the stranger Lana had befriended. It was time for him to go home to his small quarters in the cottage at the far end of the property, but tomorrow Santo would know what to do.

In another part of the villa, Lana and Peter were getting to know each other intimately.

Chapter Ten

Santo lay in bed, having barely slept three hours, his mind preoccupied with protecting the young countess. He could tell that it was dawn, noticing rays of early sunlight sneak into his room through the small cracks in the Venetian blinds. He got up and walked to his laptop, placing it onto his desk. "I have to start somewhere," he thought, firing up the machine. He decided to start simply, typing 'person search' into Google. He clicked on the first result, and on the search website typed the name 'Peter Claasen'.

Santo left the computer running while he went to the kitchen to make his coffee. Patrizio was still asleep in the neighboring room of the cottage they shared. When he returned he was surprised to find that the search was complete. There were four persons by that name and the same spelling.

Opening up the first link, the man in question was a retired German automotive engineer with expertise in electronics, residing in Munich with family.

The second candidate was a twelve-year-old boy from Toronto, Canada, who had gained recognition for efforts in raising funds for a local animal shelter. "Can't be him," Santo thought, admiring the youth's sense of community.

Moving onto the next Mr. Claasen, he learned of a mathematics and chess teacher from Ohio whose student had won the junior national chess championship. The photo showed a man in his forties, bound by a wheelchair, smiling broadly with his students. Santo sighed heavily before exploring the fourth and last option.

Opening the link, he read the headline of a newspaper article: "Dutch National Vanishes after Holiday in Acapulco, Mexico". A wave of excitement ran through Santo's body. He read on.

Peter Claasen, aged 36, was last seen leaving a nightclub with two women in Acapulco. His wife states he never returned to his home in Holland as planned. After initial investigations, Mexican authorities have no reason to believe Claasen was a victim of foul play. Hotel records confirm he had checked out and, according to border security, left the country.

Santo noted the date of the article. Almost twelve months had passed. Then he looked at the photo of the Dutch national. The man's description indicated a man of athletic build, six feet in height with light brown hair and eyes. He was about to compare the photo with the image he had stored of the American on the thumb drive when there was a knock at his door. It was Patrizio.

"*Buongiorno.* What are you doing in there? We'll be late for work," he said, curious as to why Santo held the door as if concealing something.

"Nothing. I'll meet you at the villa in twenty," Santo said in a serious tone. He waited for Patrizio to leave before closing the door and returning to complete his sleuthing.

The images of both men were not dissimilar. One could easily pass for the other to the untrained eye. "It would take minor disguise," Santo thought, wondering if the two men had crossed paths. Looking at his watch, not wanting to be tardy for duty, he decided to forward this information to the Italian authorities at the first opportunity, while keeping a close eye on Lana's activities.

Chapter Eleven

Isabella gave one last stir to the saffron risotto before dishing it onto the plates from a set Nick's parents had given them as a wedding present. A green salad with a vinaigrette dressing was already on the table ready to complement the flavor of the risotto. Nick entered the kitchen looking refreshed after his routine evening shower. He smiled at her as she handed him his plate. She lit the candle and poured him a glass of Chianti.

"None for you?" he asked, noticing water in her glass.

"No, darling," she answered and proceeded to ask about the fishing trip. He ate and spoke, but Isabella was not really listening, anxious to break her good news. Finally, unable to contain herself, she rested her fork on the plate and held up her hand, gesturing "stop." She had interrupted her husband in midsentence. Although surprised, Nick obediently stopped talking.

"I'm pregnant!" she blurted out, surprising herself. "It's confirmed. I had an appointment with my gynecologist this morning after doing a home pregnancy test. I'm about four weeks along. We're having a baby."

Nick was speechless—happy but speechless. Raising his glass, he toasted her and their baby, before getting up from his chair and hugging his wife for what seemed like an eternity. It was a magical moment for both of them. They spent the rest of the evening planning their future as a family, until, exhausted from the emotional high, they fell asleep in each other's arms. Nick slept like a baby. Isabella slept fitfully. The fugitive once again invaded her dreams.

Chapter Twelve

Los Angeles, LAPD, Monday 08:00

Chief Detective Paoli had just finished introducing his sixteen-year-old niece to the head of the mail room department before returning to his office. The young girl was doing work experience, but had aspirations of becoming a journalist—a slight deviation from the family legacy of law enforcement. Carla was smart with a yearning for adventure and wisdom beyond her years. Tyrone, her supervisor, was happy to take her under his wing and have her accompany him on the morning mail delivery round.

"It's like a medication round at a hospital except we don't ask people if they are feeling better," he explained. Carla smiled and nodded, indicating that she understood and would not deviate from regulations. Their route took them past the Special Victims Unit where Nick had an office and then up to the fifth level to Detective Isabella's office. Tyrone stopped to deliver two large white envelopes to her secretary.

Just at that moment, Isabella emerged from her room to retrieve messages that Julie, her efficient personal assistant, had accumulated. Isabella smiled at Carla. For some reason the young girl reminded her of Nancy Drew. Putting that brief observation behind her, she thanked Tyrone for the mail and returned to her desk. Isabella opened one of the larger envelopes to find it contained a dossier from the US Marine Corps. It pertained to Peter Steil. Excitedly she dialed Grant's extension and invited him to meet her in Chief Paoli's office.

Detective Grant Simms had been the head of the Cold Case division in Chicago, and been reassigned to join the task force in LA to hunt down fugitives. He was single and preferred this status after watching his high school sweetheart be gunned down by thugs in a senseless drive by shooting ten years earlier. Six foot tall with sandy colored hair and dark brown eyes, he had several female admirers. Isabella was already in the chief's office when he was shown into the large room by the secretary. Isabella was excited, he could tell that much, but was unsure about what.

"After some digging and information obtained from reliable sources, Isabella has received a dossier about Peter Steil," Chief Paoli began. "I'm sure that you are familiar with the case of this man wanted for the murder of his family," he continued. Grant nodded, glancing at his female colleague.

"The US Marines have provided classified information about Steil going AWOL in Afghanistan, however for political reasons they have logged his disappearance as missing in action," Isabella announced. "They have also included contact details to a buddy that served with him, a certain Alex Cooper."

"I think it's worth paying Lieutenant Cooper a visit. He lives in San Fernando and is expecting you," Chief Paoli informed the two detectives.

After leaving the chief's office both detectives made plans to drive to San Fernando that same day. Isabella sent Nick a quick message so that he wouldn't worry if she was home later than usual. She had no plans to inform her boss or other colleagues of her current maternity status until it was absolutely necessary. Nick respected her wishes.

Chapter Thirteen

San Fernando, California

Grant and Isabella listened to classical music on the journey to Lieutenant Cooper's property. They stopped short of the gate to confirm the number on the mailbox before proceeding up the driveway to the main house, where they were met by a white boxer. The animal greeted them with enthusiasm but responded immediately to its master's command.

"Bella-Rose! Enough. Come!" The dog stopped jumping around the visitors and obeyed the sturdy-looking man standing on the porch.

"I apologize for that, but she's still a puppy," Lt. Cooper stated, inviting his guests into his modestly furnished home. They followed him into the living room where they accepted a cold iced tea from a pitcher, already on the coffee table in preparation for the meeting.

"Thank you for taking the time to meet with us," Grant began. "We will not be long, but have just a few questions."

Lt. Cooper nodded. He appeared older than his stated years, with a haunted look in his eyes that he tried to disguise with frequent smiling.

"I hope that the information I impart for your investigation will be kept confidential. I do not wish to be mentioned as a source," he stated. Grant and Isabella agreed to be discreet.

The lieutenant leaned back in his recliner, making himself comfortable, and began his account.

"There is no easy way to say this, but Peter Steil is a sociopath," he announced. "However, his personality structure made him a good and fearless soldier. He flew helicopters dangerously close to the enemy on the ground and after each mission took delight in bragging about numbers of casualties. Women and children included."

Isabella shuddered at hearing this, knowing that he would kill again if not stopped. Grant sat motionless, transfixed by the ex-marine's detailed account.

"He is not to be underestimated," Cooper continued. "To catch him you have to think like him."

"Any idea where we could find him?" Isabella asked, hoping for more clues.

"He did talk about early retirement, that he had enough funds," Cooper said, squinting his eyes as if trying to recall anything else of use. "He hated the heat of the desert, that was for sure, so he's probably hiding out somewhere with a cooler climate."

He paused and scratched his head. Isabella and Grant waited patiently for him to continue. Just as they were about to thank him for time dedicated to seeing them, the lieutenant remembered something.

"He mentioned something about a family holiday in Canada as a boy. If I was going to disappear that's where I would go. The opportunities are endless if one wants to remain incognito."

This was a seemingly insignificant detail but taking other facts into consideration, it made sense. Grant and Isabella thanked him profusely and returned to the car in hope of creating a hypothesis and their next move by the time they reached LA. If Peter had indeed fled to Canada, they would have to involve their Canadian colleagues and act quickly.

Chapter Fourteen

Nick was watching reruns of *Happy Days* when he heard the front door open. He waited for Isabella to announce her return but it was not forthcoming. Concerned, he followed her down the hall and into their bedroom.

"Everything OK?" he asked, noticing that she looked pale and exhausted. She sat on the edge of the bed before speaking.

"It was a good visit. Productive. Grant and I have some theories but I think we need FBI and possibly Interpol involvement." He waited for her to continue, but instead she stripped off and got under a hot shower.

"I'll make you something to eat," he called out, giving her time to unwind.

When she had finished toweling off, she put on her pajamas and walked into the kitchen where Nick was warming up a pot of vegetable soup. She ate in silence, dipping the bread into the soup and asking for more once she had finished. Isabella was hungry. Tired and very hungry. After dinner they sat together on the couch, where she lay her head on his shoulders and began to confide in him.

"The man is dangerous," she said, "but I need to catch him. I haven't told Paoli that I am expecting, because he will be inclined to assign someone else to the case and have me sitting behind a desk whistling Dixie all day. That would drive me crazy."

Nick caressed her hair softly, allowing her to rest and feel secure. She looked up at him as if wanting to ask him something, but then reconsidered.

"Do you want me to tell him and that I support your involvement with the investigation?" he asked, hoping that she would not perceive his offer as sexist. Isabella nodded, but indicated that she wished to be present and have Grant privy to the discussion. Tomorrow was another day with, hopefully, a good outcome for all.

Isabella slept like a baby, uninterrupted by dreams.

Chapter Fifteen

Grindelwald, Switzerland

Irma Trauber had just finished dining with her husband, Otto, in their modest suite of their hotel overlooking the township, when the phone rang. It was an internal line from reception, which at that hour usually indicated a problem. The receptionist in the lobby apologetically explained that a guest had arrived but the reservation had not been secured. Irma stepped behind the desk and welcomed Mr. Mason Sands, a news anchor from Houston, Texas here on a short vacation. He was mid-forties, six feet tall, with the looks of a handsome cattle rancher. He spoke with a southern drawl, which Irma found difficult but managed to decipher.

"I sure did make a reservation, Ma'am, six months ago to be exact. Maybe all the cold up here in the Alps froze up your computer data base," he joked. Irma smiled and chuckled while thinking of a solution before saying with a slight Germanic accent, "*Ja*, it may be so. We had a very cold winter. But not to worry, I will give you the suite reserved for my sons when they visit. It is comfortable, spacious and you get it at the price of a regular room.

Sound good?" She hoped that her enthusiasm had won over the customer.

"*Ja, Fraulein,*" the Texan replied, much obliged by the manager's generosity. He filled out the required forms, leaving a deposit with his platinum Amex credit card. Irma summoned a bellhop to escort Mason to his lodgings, before wishing the guest a restful night and enjoyable stay.

The bellhop was transfixed by the Texan's cowboy boots and hat as they traveled up to the last floor. Irma had given their new guest pamphlets of activities that may be of interest, which he was studying as they rode the elevator.

"This looks interesting," he remarked, showing the bellhop a picture of helicopter tours. The boy nodded and smiled, trying hard not to laugh at the visitor's accent.

Once in the suite, Mason tipped the boy generously, then locked the door behind him and rang his wife, Lilly, letting her know he had arrived safely. Lilly had been unable to accompany him on this trip due to her own work commitments. He set up his laptop so that he could keep abreast of current affairs in the world and back home, then showered and went to sleep.

The following day Mason boarded the helicopter with five other enthusiasts to tour the great mountains described in the brochure. Peter Claasen was their pilot and guide. Mason sat next to him in the copilot seat. He was encouraged by having another fellow American to communicate with for the duration of the flight. He found Peter to be easygoing and even charming toward the ladies on the tour, but not as forthcoming as most fellow countrymen would be on his background.

That evening Mason wrote to his wife to tell her about the helicopter tour he had enjoyed, uploading pictures of the journey. The first day of his vacation had been a good one.

Chapter Sixteen

Chief Paoli, Isabella, Nick and Grant sat around the oval table in the conference room. After sharing the information gathered from Lt. Cooper, the chief invited Ed Smith, head of the FBI division, to join them by video conference. Isabella thought that the man looked like he had been sleep deprived for a decade given the gauntness in appearance. Nevertheless, he spoke eloquently and with authority.

"We have several possible leads on the whereabouts of fugitive Peter Steil," he declared, and proceeded to give an account provided by the first source. An image of security footage from a party, or what seemed to the detectives like a high society gathering, appeared on the monitor. Isabella recognized Peter. They were also provided with the additional information of the missing Dutch national, which they studied closely.

"That's him," she said without faltering or averting her gaze from the screen. He had lost some weight and changed his appearance slightly but she was sure it was him.

"OK, interesting, because he was also sighted in Mexico and Alaska by some local tourists and at a small hotel in Canada by a skiing instructor. These sightings are in response to local police sending out a bulletin for this man's capture," Ed Smith continued. "The problem is that the time frames of these sightings are mostly around the time of this footage we are looking at."

"What do you suggest?" Chief Paoli asked his senior colleague. "We will need more man power and intelligence for positive identification before swooping in for the arrest."

"I am positive that the man on the screen is Peter Steil," Isabella said with certainty.

"Every lead will need to be followed, so yes I agree that we need to approach this hunt methodically and proactively," Ed Smith asserted.

The group decided to put together several teams to investigate the leads and confirm Steil's whereabouts in preparation for an arrest. Ed Smith told the detectives that his source for the video footage of the party was a member of a private security detail, a certain Santo Mancini, who had connections in the area and could be of value. Smith agreed to liaise with Steven Politzski, the head of Interpol, to be a conduit for additional intel with the use of his contacts in Italy and Switzerland.

"We need a team up in Canada, Alaska and Mexico," Chief Paoli started. He looked at Isabella. "I want you to go to Mexico."

Isabella was stunned. Her instincts drew her to look at the Swiss Alps option.

"I think I would be better off following the lead this Santo has provided," she said, determined not to be dissuaded. "What am I doing in Mexico?"

"There may be a connection between the disappearance of the Dutch tourist, Peter Claasen, and the man in the footage in Milan, who, according to our source, goes by the same name," he explained.

"The Mexican authorities don't seem to think there has been foul play, according to the newspaper article, so why would we bother with that?" Isabella asked, having made up her mind about what she was not prepared to do. The chief said nothing, but was not impressed with her insubordination. The atmosphere in the room was tense.

"What do we know about this Santo Mancini, anyway? And how do we know he hasn't got his own agenda, maybe ratting the fugitive out after a disagreement of sorts?" Grant asked, trying to support Isabella as well as avoid diversion off-topic. "The article states the tourist was seen leaving the club with two men. Maybe they were in it together. You know, hatching a plan to help Peter vanish for a tidy sum of money."

"Chief," Ed Smith interrupted, addressing Paoli. "I don't mean to tell you how to conduct business, but I think the best way forward is to follow this lead. Santo's background check has already been cleared by the Bureau, although we still have to consider any possibility of deception. You have the advantage of a preliminary positive ID by someone on your team, so let's box clever on this."

Chief Paoli nodded in agreement. Isabella and Grant smiled at each other. The meeting ended with rough plans on how to bring the investigation to a definitive conclusion. Isabella was satisfied with the outcome, but was dreading the next part of the meeting with her boss.

The chief returned to sit behind his desk, and was surprised to find that his colleagues hadn't moved.

There was a knock at the door before the topic of family planning could commence. It was Carla. Once invited, she entered the conference room pushing a trolley of pastries and beverages, and handed a parcel to her uncle. Chief Paoli thanked his niece, escorting her to the door.

"We have to inform you that we are pregnant," Nick announced, assuming the girl had left.

"Congratulations," Chief Paoli responded sincerely.

"This shouldn't change the team selected for the capture of Steil," Nick continued.

"Oh but sure it does. I am not having her"—he glanced at Isabella—"gallivanting around the Alps in pursuit of a dangerous criminal in a fragile state." His voice had risen a decibel at 'fragile'.

"Mom went tracking in Japan when she was expecting me," a gentle voice announced from behind them. They turned to find Carla standing at the door, her expression one of innocence and solidarity for the older female detective. It made Isabella smile.

"Please, Carla, don't you have stamps to count?" her uncle asked impatiently.

"I'm only saying that just 'cause a woman is pregnant doesn't mean she can't still do stuff," Carla offered. Then she was gone. Chief Paoli closed the door and turned to his team. Isabella, Grant and Nick now stood with folded arms in front of their boss. Chief Paoli studied Isabella, who he suddenly noticed looked beautiful. He kicked himself for not noticing how glowing she looked earlier and figuring it out for himself.

"How far along are you?" he asked.

"About five weeks."

"OK. I will keep you on the taskforce, but we need to have a contingency plan in the event it gets too dangerous or you feel unwell."

All were in agreement. It was time to get this long-awaited show on the road.

Chapter Seventeen

Milan, Italy, Bar Terraci, 20:00

Santo and Patrizio sat opposite one another in the corner of the small coffee shop. They had just finished drinking espressos, something that was not unusual at that time of night for most Italians.

"So, what is this all about? I hope you aren't going to trick me into going out on a blind date again," Patrizio asked his good friend and colleague of many years. Their fathers had been coworkers at the Banco d'Italia and both had been involved in coaching soccer on the weekends, which is how Santo and Patrizio had first met as boys. After completing their compulsory military service, they joined the armed forces, finding work as protective detail for the elite of society.

Santo kept a serious demeanor, until eventually he spoke.

"I need someone I can trust for an assignment," he began. "This conversation is absolutely confidential, understood?"

Patrizio, somewhat amused by the air of mystery, answered, "Ooh, the mysterious Signor Santo," and leaned forward, drawing closer to his buddy.

"I am not joking. Are you with me or not? I have to know before I give up details," Santo retorted impatiently.

"Of course. I swear on the Bible. You can take me into your confidence," his friend replied, now more serious and with sincerity.

"Do you remember the night at Contessa Safini's party, when I asked you to store footage?" Patrizio nodded. "Well, I had a gut feeling about one of the guests. Don't ask me how or why," Santo continued, raising his hand to make the point, "but it turns out that the American may be wanted in the United States."

Patrizio remained silent waiting for more. Santo swirled his empty espresso cup.

"After forwarding the USB to Interpol in Washington, D.C., I got a call from Agent Stefano Boccetti here in Milan." Santo paused before continuing. "Steven Politzski, the head of Interpol, has been having conversations with the LA police department and FBI concerning a certain fugitive," he explained.

"The man at the party?" Patrizio asked, to confirm that he was following the thread. Santo nodded.

"A task force is being put together to capture him, but we need to assist in tracking him when he is with the countess. Also, his identity will need confirming before an arrest can be made. The authorities here in Milan have formally asked for our help."

"What do we need to do?" Patrizio asked, hoping Santo had a plan.

"I am working on something. The man's name is Peter Steil, but he goes by Peter Claasen. A real social parasite. I am sure he will make use of Lana Safini. So far I have placed a tracking device on her cars. I will keep in touch and we can reconvene here in a couple of days."

Santo got up to put on his coat. Before leaving the venue, he turned to his colleague, reminding him that the information was classified.

Patrizio sat for a moment, digesting the facts. Santo had placed a lot of trust in him, which he would not betray. They were almost like brothers. A young waitress cleared the small table and smiled at the generous tip Santo had left tucked under the saucer. He smiled back at her, before leaving to head home. It had been a very long day.

Chapter Eighteen

Grindelwald, Tourist Center

Peter was preparing a cup of coffee in the clubhouse kitchenette when Bruno walked up to the counter. "You have a visitor," he announced and winked. Before he could reply, the young countess stood in the doorway. Concealing his irritation at the impromptu visit, he greeted her with a strong embrace, before asking, "What brings you here? How did you find me?"

"I have my sources," Lana replied, an answer that did not sit well with him. "I wanted to spend some alone time with you as well as to invite you to a charity polo match in Vienna next weekend."

"That sounds very romantic," he mustered. "I would like that very much. How did you get here?" he asked, hoping that nobody had followed her. Wrapping her arms around his neck and pulling him closer for a kiss, she simply indicated that it was none of his concern. "This woman is interesting," Peter thought, hoping that he would not have to dispose of her too soon.

They spent the evening at his cabin, Peter putting his charm on display, playing the perfect host, while mentally planning for possible unwanted scenarios that could jeopardize his future. A characteristic of a sociopath was to be able to compartmentalize, and it was something Peter Steil did well. Too well.

Less than a mile from the cabin, Santo sat in his four wheel drive hoping that no harm would befall the young and naïve aristocrat. She was oblivious to having been tailed.

He had entrusted the authorities with the images on the USB, hoping that it would assist them in bringing about justice. Santo longed to have a change in career path—he did not want to be remain in his current role until the day he retired. He was a man with realistic ambitions. For now, he allowed himself the luxury of fantasizing about his future.

Chapter Nineteen

Los Angeles Police Department, 11:00

Carla had been entrusted to conduct the morning mail delivery round. It was her third week of work experience at the department, which she was thoroughly enjoying. Passing Isabella's office, she quickly glanced at the detective deep in conversation on the phone. Carla admired the woman and was pleased to hear that her uncle, Chief Paoli, had sanctioned her ongoing involvement in the investigation. "Chasing a fugitive in a foreign country. How exciting!" the girl thought.

Isabella replaced the receiver and noticed Carla. She smiled at the young girl as she passed her and her trolley, making her way to the chief's office for what was considered to be a very important and classified meeting.

The office was full and Isabella could see they had been enjoying light conversation accompanied by coffee and doughnuts while waiting for her to join them. She recognized a handful of people before being introduced to Special Agent Claudia Conti.

"Special Agent Conti, let me introduce Detective Isabella Ashford-Hauser. She has had involvement in this case from the very beginning and will fill you in on the details later," the chief offered politely.

Isabella and the new agent shook hands.

"Agent Conti is FBI and will accompany you on your quest, along with Detective Simms," he concluded. Grant smiled at his colleague as she looked over.

"Call me Claudia. I have heard many good things about you," Conti stated.

"I look forward to working with you," Isabella responded sincerely, already liking the new member of the team. Claudia was of Italian origin, proficient in five languages, including Russian, and had worked hard to join ranks with the FBI. She was of the same height and build as Isabella, with shoulder-length black hair pulled back in a ponytail, tanned complexion and almond shaped light brown eyes.

"We have our Interpol colleagues joining us online by video conference," Chief Paoli said, turning toward the screen where Steven Politzski, Agent Mia Strauss, the Swiss contact and Stefano Boccetti from Italy starred back at them.

"Good morning ladies and gentlemen," Steven, the head of Interpol, greeted them in a matter of fact manner. He went on to introduce his other colleagues to the American detectives, with Chief Paoli returning the courtesy.

"As you are aware," Steven reiterated, "we have reason to believe that Mr. Steil is in Switzerland, but has been traveling around Europe with false identification under the alias Peter Claasen. The source of this information has provided a USB with pictures of our man." Just then photos of the fugitive flashed onto the screen. "He has become friendly with the daughter of Count Safini, Lana Safini. Fortunately for us, our informant is Santo Mancini, part of the family's private security detail."

"So how do we find this Santo?" Grant asked "and how do we know if Lana Safini is not in collusion with our man?" Grant found this all too simplistic. Something did not compute.

"Santo has already placed tracking devices on her cars and she appears to have gone to a little skiing resort in the Swiss Alps, called Grindelwald," Agent Mia Strauss informed. "We think he is working as a helicopter pilot for the tourist bureau."

Chief Paoli thanked the agents for the information, promising to reconvene once he and his crew had formulated a plan of action. The video link ended.

"This just confirms what Lieutenant Cooper alluded to in reference to Steil's preferred climatic choice, hence his possible whereabouts," Isabella said, looking at Grant, who nodded.

"I think we should meet tomorrow morning with some ideas and put the plan in motion. You two ladies should become better acquainted over lunch," Chief Paoli encouraged the two female agents, after escorting his team to the conference room door.

It was settled. Finally the mission was taking shape.

Chapter Twenty

Claudia and Isabella took the chief's advice and ordered Japanese takeout, which they enjoyed back in Isabella's office. They shared some of their personal experiences relating to their backgrounds as well as their chosen careers. Claudia was easy to talk to, volunteering information about growing up with traditional Italian parents in a fast-growing modern America.

Their attention was drawn back to the case when Grant appeared at the door. He seemed enthusiastic. The women exchanged glances, inviting him to join their private buffet. Grant sat next to Claudia, who started preparing a platter for him.

"I have a great idea!" he announced, almost too loudly. They sat quietly, inviting him to disclose his epiphany. "We are going to go to this Grindelwald place undercover!"

"Tell us more," Claudia encouraged.

"We," he said, indicating to himself and Isabella, "will pose as newlyweds staying at a resort and we can do a bit of snooping around. That way, we can keep an eye on

Mr. Steil or Claasen or whatever he calls himself. We can confirm his identity. Then we can place him under arrest and—"

Claudia had raised her hand, interrupting him before he could say any more. Grant looked at her confused.

"We need means to positively confirm his identity with either DNA or fingerprints and the like. That part of the plan has to be orchestrated meticulously," she remarked. Isabella was on her third helping of Teriyaki chicken but nodded in agreement with her new friend. Grant sipped on miso soup, saying nothing. Agent Conti considered Grant's little plan of charades.

"So, you're newlyweds, and who am I supposed to be, the maid?' Claudia asked, leaning forward in her chair. Isabella intercepted to stop what she sensed to be a brewing storm.

"We're all here working together, let's not forget that, please," she affirmed. "You both have valid points. The way we plan this and play our roles is going to be paramount to avoiding mistakes and catching him. Now, I'm happy to be Grant's fake wife, while you Claudia, can be our eyes and ears of what's going on in the wings. Your sleuthing will be much appreciated."

The young FBI agent smiled, then said, "I know for a fact that we have a record of Peter's fingerprints on file from his marine days. We'll get something to compare them with so let's not get banana shaped about that detail yet." Then the young agent stood and walked around to Isabella's computer.

"Let's start planning a honeymoon," she volunteered.

"We'll need false identification," Grant announced, contributing to the plan. Isabella, Grant and Claudia worked tirelessly for the next few hours on what would hopefully be a great scheme for deception and capture.

Chapter Twenty-One

Grindelwald, Kirbana Hotel, 18:00

Mason Sands returned from his hiking trip that had taken him into the forest of the surrounding mountains. As he was unlocking the door to the suite, he heard the telephone in his room ringing.

It was the hotel switchboard connecting a call from his wife. It was good to hear her voice. They hadn't been married long, but they had a special 'ESP connection', as Lilly Sands would say.

"Honey, great to hear from you!" he exclaimed.

"I've been missing you," she replied. "We all have. How are things?"

"Things are just great here, darlin'. Did you get the pictures from the flight I took?" he asked, hoping that there had been no problem with the Wi-Fi.

"I did, thank you Mr. Adventurous," she teased.

"I went hiking today and am wasted. I think I'll upload the photos from today for you and then call it a night."

"A warm bath and a plate of hot goulash is just what you need" she advised, knowing that he would be more inclined to eat a bag of potato chips washed down with a Pepsi for dinner and call it a 'stable diet'.

"Good night, honey. Speak to you soon," he said, blowing kisses into the receiver before hanging up. Mason was truly enjoying his break from the fast pace of the city. It was peaceful, or so he thought.

Chapter Twenty-Two

Vienna, Austria

The G-6 was on final approach with clearance to land. Peter sighed with relief as he felt the wheels make contact with the runway. He had wanted to drive to Austria to avoid complications, but Lana had sent her private jet to pick him up. Peter had flown his chopper to Bern airport where he caught the luxury jet. Disembarking from the aircraft with a small suitcase in his hand, he caught sight of the limousine waiting for him. The chauffeur was a young man who looked barely eighteen.

The car drove along the outskirts of Vienna, its rich culture evidenced by the Baroque architecture. Hans, the young driver, did not speak unless spoken to, which was just fine with Peter. Hans studied his passenger using the rearview mirror while stopped at traffic lights. He did not care for him, but kept his thoughts to himself.

The gates of the small palace were opened by remote control from inside the guard tower. A security guard waved the car through, directing it up the long driveway. Hans stopped the vehicle in front of and parallel to the main entrance. He opened the passenger door and waited for the visitor to alight. Without thanking his young but efficient driver, Peter walked up to the entrance where Lana awaited him.

"Oh, my darling," she cried, throwing herself into his arms. "I'm so grateful you could join us!"

She led him into the foyer of the palace and introduced him to her parents, Count and Countess Safini. This was too much for him. He hoped that Lana would not surprise him with news that she was expecting a baby and wanted to be married. For him it was only sex, nothing more, and he knew he should have been more careful. Charming and a good actor, he played along, feigning empathy or enthusiasm when needed.

A valet brought Peter's suitcase to the room allocated to him for the weekend. The valet left, and Lana seductively pointed out the door that led to her own adjoining apartment. Peter hid his disdain and was saved by a servant appearing with an itinerary of the festivities and times for presentation to various events and meals. "This is like being in the marines again," he thought, but at least the structure would be a good excuse not to spend too much time alone with Lana. He was regretting accepting the invitation, but she was a means to an end. For now having her around suited him.

He ushered Lana out on the pretense of needing to freshen up, locked both doors for privacy, and sat on the king sized canopy bed to study the itinerary. He would cope. He had to.

Chapter Twenty-Three

Houston, Texas, 20:00

Lilly Sands relaxed on the couch after a long day at the office. It was time for her favorite TV show on real crime and unsolved mysteries. She pressed the button on the remote until she reached the correct channel. Normally Mason would watch with her, but he was on vacation with a view of other interesting things. Lilly smiled at the thought of her beloved nursing blisters on his feet after a long hike. He was prone to feet problems but that did not deter him from being fully active. His job as a news anchor was too sedentary for such a restless spirit as him.

The show finally started after a series of advertisements on junk food. She smiled again, reminded of his habits.

Several cases of unsolved crimes were showcased until the last set of ads, when Lilly decided to have another cup of ginger tea. The show's presenter described a case of triple homicide and mistaken identity. Lilly was fascinated and studied the composite sketch closely. There was a familiarity to the face on the screen. She dismissed it, thinking she was just becoming confused by the barrage of mugshots. "After a while, they all look the same," she thought, turning the set off and heading to bed.

Her dreams were mostly pleasant, filled with images of Mason climbing Mount Fuji years earlier, drinking beer at a family gathering, their honeymoon in Hawaii. Then the images became blurred with Mason trying to warn her of something she could not see. Lilly woke suddenly, her heart pounding, sweat making her nightgown cling to her body. She got out of bed and showered. Feeling better in a fresh nightgown, Lilly returned to bed and drifted off to a more restful sleep.

Chapter Twenty-four

Vienna, Safini Residence

Peter joined the hunting party outside the stables that afternoon. The count had taken it upon himself to show his daughter's friend around the grounds and introduced him to the stable hands. He had decided that Peter would be riding alongside him and the other select aristocrats who partook in the seasonal hunting activities. Peter borrowed a spare riding outfit the count had set aside for him.

"Meet Rio," Count Safini said, introducing the young stallion to his guest. Peter smiled as he caressed the animal's forehead. Rio jerked back initially and had to be persuaded to accept Peter as his rider for the afternoon. A bribe in the form of sugar cubes did the trick. Count Tommaso Tomei and Baron Giorgio Emanuele joined Peter and their host at the edge of the property.

"My other hunting partners are reserving their strength for an all-night celebration and tomorrow's polo event. I hope it will raise money to contribute to the restoration of the oncology wing of the main hospital," Count Safini explained. Peter nodded, hiding his urge to laugh at the lame concept. The hunting dogs were getting restless, prompting the count to initiate the event with the traditional blowing of the horn. The hunt for pheasants had begun.

Peter, with his military background, was an excellent marksman, much to everyone's surprise. For him, it felt good to have a legitimate reason to kill something. At the end of the afternoon ten pheasants had been collected. The count and his party returned to the palace to prepare for the evening's festivities.

"You surprise me, Peter," Safini said as they walked into the foyer. "I didn't know you had such great aim. In fact I don't know much about you other than your making my daughter very happy," he continued. "We shall get better acquainted this weekend."

To Peter, it sounded like an order, and he did not like this one bit. First he had to deal with a clingy woman, and now the father was getting a bit too intense for his liking.

But the evening went better than Peter had expected. After dinner he excused himself, claiming to have a headache. Lana followed him to his room, but Peter stopped her from entering. After an apologetic explanation of his sudden state and a promise that the following day would be different, she conceded and respected his need for rest.

Peter locked the door behind him and took a cold shower before climbing into the gigantic bed. "Alone at last," he thought.

Downstairs in the large dining room the table was being cleared by servants. The men had retired to the library for Cognac and cigars. Lana joined her mother in the drawing room, where they drank tea and played chess. Princess, the family beagle, sat quietly at their feet.

"Peter seems like such a gentleman," her mother began. "How long have you known him?". Lana provided her with just enough information to satisfy initial curiosity.

"I hope to get to know him better. We don't know much about him, and neither do you," the countess remarked. It was true, she didn't know much at all. Lana hoped that this would soon change.

Chapter Twenty-Five

Santo Mancini and Patrizio Palazzi sat opposite each other in the small living room of the modest quarters at the northeast end of the Viennese Safini property. They had both observed Peter's arrival and witnessed his expertise with a firearm on the hunting expedition earlier that afternoon. It worried them that such a dangerous man could disguise himself so well, mingling with prominent people and manipulating them to believe whatever he chose fit.

"What do we do now?" Patrizio asked Santo, wishing they could just tackle the man to the ground and beat the life out of him.

"We have to await orders," he replied, aware of his friend's growing impatience. "But tomorrow, we can use the opportunity to take something he touches, to lift finger prints and forward it to the FBI," Santo promised.

"And then what?" Patrizio queried. "Where is the taskforce from the US? Are we just going to wait until he eludes capture again?" His voice rose as he went on, feeling frustrated by a sense of disempowerment.

Santo looked at his friend, reassuring him that they had an important role to play and that the element of surprise was the best weapon in battle. Peter Steil didn't know they were here and onto him.

It was true. Peter, clouded by arrogance, was ignorant of this very fact.

Chapter Twenty-Six

It had been a laborious week for Isabella and her colleagues of planning disguises, working on false cover stories and fine tuning their strategies in preparation to capture Peter Steil, aka Peter Claasen.

Isabella was preparing for bed, after packing what seemed to her husband to be her entire wardrobe.

"You sure you're coming back to me?' he teased.

"Count on it, babe," she replied. "We are having a baby, remember?" she teased back.

"How are you feeling? What did the doctor say?" Nick asked, his tone more serious.

"She said to take it easy and not run after any criminals," Isabella joked, but seeing concern in her husband's eyes, quickly added, "I am sorry Nick. I've been given the all clear. I promise to take the supplements, eat like a horse and not partake in any shootouts."

Nick knew that it would be pointless to try and persuade his wife to reconsider the mission. He was worried even though she seemed strong, both psychologically and physically since the morning sickness had subsided.

She climbed into bed and snuggled up against his chest. His heartbeat was a steady rhythm which, like a lullaby, helped her drift off to sleep. For once, her dreams were not frightening.

Chapter Twenty-Seven

Vienna, Safini Residence

Peter looked at himself in the mirror, cringing inwardly at the costume the count had picked for him to attend the charity ball. He was dressed as a Musketeer. It would have been seen as incredibly rude to decline wearing the outfit, so he obliged, hoping that he would be able to disappear during the evening feigning another migraine. Lana knocked at the door, entering the room before being invited to.

"You look so handsome, Peter," she commented, again throwing herself at him. They kissed.

"Thank you, my darling, and you look stunning," he said, returning the compliment. She did look good in the princess outfit she had chosen.

Together they descended the winding staircase to join the other guests in the ballroom. Count Safini smiled at him—a clear sign of approval. The young couple mingled with their guests, with Peter on his best behavior throughout the evening.

The day's polo event had attracted many horse lovers of high society, raising a healthy sum to support the new oncology wing of the general hospital in Vienna. Peter thought it was a waste of money, and was of the opinion that these people were destined to die, so why bother investing in them? He kept his thoughts hidden well.

The evening was filled with laughter, good food and expensive wines from all over the world. Peter didn't care much for the Dom Pérignon, but drank it to ease his discomfort at being in the company of people he considered useless. Lana danced with several of the male guests, which did not bother Peter, much to Lana's annoyance. Count Tommaso Tomei and his Swedish wife, Selma, noticed him sitting alone on the balcony overlooking the vast fields. Together they approached, hoping to learn more about him. The count was a shrewd business man who saw opportunities and took them without hesitation. Peter admired this. The Swedish countess was a gentle soul, contented with supporting charities, such as the one celebrated this evening.

From afar, to Santo and Patrizio, their subject seemed to be having a good time. They had noticed that Peter had been drinking from various glass vessels, and it would be up to them to seek out the moment to collect one without drawing attention. The moment finally came. Peter had discarded a champagne flute onto a tray carried by one of the waiters. Patrizio skillfully removed it as the wait staff walked past him. Placing the glass in an evidence bag, he proudly carried it back to their quarters.

Santo shortly thereafter joined his colleague, who was sitting on the couch looking pleased with himself. Santo hated to burst his bubble, so proceeded gently.

"The man was wearing gloves. A part of his ridiculous costume, in case you hadn't noticed," Santo started, "so no fingerprints can be lifted."

Patrizio leaped off the couch, and in frustration let out several profanities, most of which were in Italian. Suddenly he stopped his tirade, and turning to face Santo he said, "We can get DNA, right? That counts for something."

"Sure, but we need something to compare it to. I'm afraid I don't think we have that yet," Santo concluded.

"We will," Patrizio replied, convinced that it would only be a matter of time before their man slipped up. He placed a call to Agent Stefano Boccetti, who gave him further instructions on how to proceed.

Santo returned to the party, leaving his friend to finalize plans with the agent.

Chapter Twenty-Eight

Houston, Texas

Lilly Sands packed her briefcase and joined her colleague in the elevator. After a long day's work as an executive secretary of a small insurance company, she was ready for a quiet and relaxing evening.

"Are you going to watch more crime series or have you had your dose for the week?" her colleague asked teasingly as they rode the elevator.

"I think I'll read a book tonight, a thriller, of course," she replied casually. Once they had reached the lobby, they wished each other a good evening and went their separate ways.

In truth, Lilly had been bothered by the last case on the crime show the night before. Thankfully, she was in the habit of recording shows of interest in the event of her falling asleep midway, which was not an infrequent occurrence.

The drive home was uneventful. She secured the car in the spacious garage and walked into the lovely home she shared with her beloved husband, Mason. Photos of family and friends decorated the mantelpiece in the living room. She showered, heated up a ready-made meal in the microwave and pulled up the recording from the previous night's show.

Studying the image of the triple murder suspect, she noted again a familiarity about him. Instinctively, she retrieved the photos Mason had sent her from Switzerland and began to study them. The helicopter pilot featured in one of the pictures. Most of his face was obscured by his shades and the headset, with the microphone concealing his mouth. The striking similarity was the shape of the chin with its prominent cleft and small mole on the right side of the nose.

She recalled that Mason had mentioned the pilot as an interesting character, almost secretive and not willing to disclose personal information about where he was from, although Mason had been able to tell by his accent that the pilot was North American. As she made a cup of tea, Lilly considered the time difference in the Swiss Alps. It was not too late to call her husband.

Chapter Twenty-Nine

Thirty-thousand feet above the Atlantic Ocean, the 747 American airliner glided effortlessly through the air. Isabella, Grant, and FBI agent Claudia Conti sat abeam the large wing on the starboard side of the aircraft. Isabella took the aisle seat due to the need to mobilize and use the lavatory more frequently in her gravid state. The movie selection was average, but still entertaining. The food was better than anticipated, with of course the mother-to-be requesting extra servings of everything. They slept, spoke of the strategy concerning the mission and tried to keep Claudia distracted from her fear of flying. They would land in Bern, rent a car and make their way to Grindelwald. The trio were a good match both in terms of experience and skill mix, and despite an initial rough start between Grant and Claudia, they proved to be temperamentally compatible.

Isabella looked out the window, noticing the beautiful crimson color of the sky at that altitude as they crossed time zones. She thought of her family that had perished years earlier in Mexico, wondering if this would be what Heaven was like. She closed her eyes, drifting off to sleep to the gentle hum of the airplane's four very large engines.

Chapter Thirty

Grindelwald, Kirbana Hotel

Peter was relieved to be back in his comfort zone, free of the clutches of Lana and her family. They had tried to persuade him to prolong his visit at the chateau, to no avail. Lana was disappointed that her beau was leaving her behind and had not offered to travel back to Switzerland with him. "She will get over it," he shrugged to himself on his journey home.

For reasons unknown to him, Peter had a desire to visit the Kirbana Hotel, sit at the bar nursing a Scotch on the rocks and touch base with Irma, the manager. He parked the Jeep in the carpark in the VIP spot, and walked through the front entrance. He *was* VIP, he thought. If it hadn't been for his services, the tourist industry at this time of year would be non-existent.

He walked across the lobby toward the entrance of the main bar when a familiar face took him by surprise. He immediately recognized the Texan from one of his scenic flights. The man was engrossed in a hushed phone conversation and had his laptop open. Peter, now curious, approached the man from behind while still remaining concealed by a pillar. Peering from behind the structure he did not like what he saw. Comparison photos of himself on the screen, one in the helicopter taken a few days earlier, the other from a crime show. "Shit!" he thought. The desire for a drink was strong but for self-preservation it was much stronger.

Peter stood very still behind the large pillar as Mason ended the call with his wife, closed the laptop and returned it into its designated case. He edged out to watch his subject move toward the elevator. He had to act quickly.

Peter moved up the stairs, checking each floor before moving to the next, in order to intercept Mason and to follow him back to his room. Finally, he found the Texan on the last floor, moving to a corner room at the end of the corridor. A waiter exited one of the other rooms with a tray of dishes from a room service order. An idea came to Peter.

Rushing, he caught the elevator down to the basement where staff uniforms were kept. Donning a waiter's jacket, he made his way once again via the stairs to Mason's suite. He had a plan of attack. "Thank God for my military training," he thought.

Mason was reviewing photos when he heard a knock at the door. Placing his drink on the small coffee table, he made his way to open it.

"Who is it?" he called out, nearing his attacker on the other side of the partition.

"Room service, sir," the voice said. Mason stopped in his tracks, wondering where he had heard that familiar voice. Curious, he continued and opened the door.

Peter heard the latch being shifted. He held the tray high enough to cover his face. The door opened and without hesitation the intruder entered the room.

"I didn't order anything," Mason stated, amused and surprised.

"Compliments from the hotel," came the reply.

The door closed behind them, and that's when Peter attacked swiftly and skillfully. The aim was to kill. Mason didn't have a chance.

Chapter Thirty-One

The taxi pulled up in front of the Kirbana Hotel. The driver assisted the trio with their baggage by carrying it to the main entrance, where a porter took carriage of it. Isabella and Grant had rehearsed their roles. They were newlyweds Mr. and Mrs. Simms from San Francisco. Agent Conti was not introduced as their maid, as she had feared. In fact, she would not be introduced at all. She was a skiing instructor scoping out the slopes in preparation for the next winter season.

Entering the lobby a few minutes after Isabella and Grant, in order to give the staff the impression of being a lone traveler, she waited seemingly patiently in line to be served. She watched as Irma Strauber summoned the concierge to escort the happy couple to their room once their registration had been finalized.

The manager stood behind the large counter smiling at Isabella as they waited for the concierge. Finally, clasping her hands together she exclaimed, "Congratulations!" This took Isabella and her 'husband' by surprise.

"What do you mean?" Isabella asked, perplexed.

"But *ja*, you are with child," she remarked, as if stating the obvious although Isabella was not even showing.

"How do you know?" Grant asked, curious, exchanging glances with his 'wife'.

"My dear, it is written all over you. You are glowing like a Christmas tree."

The 'newlyweds' were silent.

"And soon she will look like a Christmas pudding," a voice remarked from behind them.

They turned to find Special Agent Conti staring back at them, apparently pleased with her comment. Isabella raised an eyebrow at her as if to say, "Seriously, are you now playing the role of an arrogant guest or what?" Irma, unimpressed by the intrusion, continued by saying, "Otto is my husband and head Chef here. He comes from a long line of cooks for Royalty dating back to Marie Antoinette. I will make sure he takes good care of you and the baby, yes?" Before the mother-to-be could show any gratitude, the agent fired off another rude remark.

"We can all look forward to that!" Then, glancing at her Tissot watch, she said with impatience, "Can you please hurry this cozy rendezvous up? I haven't got all week!"

The Simms thanked Irma and followed the young concierge to their room.

Agent Conti stepped forward to check in. Irma apologetically informed her that the allocated room had a "plumbing problem" and that the only room left was on the ground floor next to the kitchen. Sensing a protest coming her way, she added, "If that is not suitable perhaps I can recommend another hotel." The agent reflected for a moment before choosing to stay at the same lodgings as her colleagues. They had a mission planned. She accepted the room, which turned out to be small, without a view, but had a comfortable bed. The manager had made a point.

Later she texted Isabella to apologize for any embarrassment she may have caused, explaining that it was the role she had given herself. Isabella, cognizant of the intention, reassured Claudia that it was the perfect cover. They arranged to meet in the morning at a local bakery to discuss their plan. Isabella and Grant wanted to make contact with their Interpol colleagues before making the move.

As Isabella settled into the comfortable twin bed, she thought of the odd scent that permeated the corridor as they walked to their room. A sweet odor. She realized it was the scent of death.

Chapter Thirty-Two

Switzerland, Friday night

Peter had returned to the safety of his cabin, where he poured himself a double Scotch on the rocks. He was sure to have covered his tracks, not leaving any evidence that could be traced back to him. Sitting in the recliner, he allowed himself to relax. All he had to do was go about his daily business. He knew that he shouldn't drink alcohol within eight hours of commencing duty as a pilot in command of the helicopter. This was a Civil Aviation Safety Authority regulation mandated to be respected. Tonight he didn't care. He needed to unwind. This was the only way he knew how.

Chapter Thirty-Three

Houston, Texas, Friday 06:00

Lilly was startled awake by a nightmare. Looking at the time, she quickly calculated that it was 12::30 p.m. in Switzerland. Concerned that she had not heard from Mason for over twenty-four hours, she decided to call his cell phone. It had been switched off and went straight to voicemail. She left a message. An hour later she left another, until that evening when she still had no word from him, which was highly unusual, she called the hotel.

"No, madam, I have not seen him, but I have just started my shift," the young staff member at the hotel reception explained. At the insistence of the distressed caller, she agreed to try the room extension. There was no reply. The receptionist reconnected the call with Lilly and requested that she call back in twenty minutes to give her enough time to check the room. Lilly agreed. It was the longest twenty minutes of Lilly's life.

The receptionist called her manager, Irma, who agreed to accompany her to investigate. As they approached the room, a sweet but offensive odor wafted into their nostrils. "This can't be good" Irma thought, but said nothing, not wanting to alarm the younger lady. She unlocked the door and tentatively pushed it open. There was nothing, but now the smell was stronger.

"Wait here," Irma instructed her staff member before entering the room to investigate further. The young lady nodded, almost relieved by the request. Irma entered the bathroom. There on the floor lay the naked body of Mason. Irma was shocked by the sight, and clasped both hands over her mouth just in time to smother her scream. Closing her eyes, she steadied her breathing, before calmly walking back out into the corridor.

"Shall I call the wife?" she asked Irma, hoping naively that nothing untoward had happened to their guest.

"No," Irma began slowly. Her face was white. "I think we should call the police first."

The two women secured the suite, and together informed the authorities and thereafter Mrs. Mason herself. It was not an easy task telling someone on the other side of the world that their loved one was no more. A difficult task, but it was Irma's.

Chapter Thirty-four

Bern, Switzerland

Mia Strauss, in her early forties, had worked for Interpol in Switzerland for the last three years. In spite of the dangers, she loved her job. She enjoyed working together with other agents located in different parts of the globe. Courtesy of the modern technology of video calls, she could put a face to the name of every colleague, making her feel part of a large team.

Her current assignment involved tracking and providing intelligence to her American colleagues concerning a fugitive, Peter Steil. Mia sat in a small coffee shop awaiting a call from Italy. Finally, her cell phone rang.

"Hello?" Mia answered.

"*Buongiorno.* Am I speaking to Mia?" the male caller asked in a strong Italian accent.

"Yes, you are," she replied, stirring her coffee.

"Ah, good. I am Stefano, your contact from Italy," he announced.

"I've been waiting for your call. I hope there is a lead," she said hopefully.

"Yes, Mia, there is. I have information of the location of your man."

"How reliable is the information?" she asked cautiously.

"Very. I have the location from security personnel who work for Count Safini," he explained. Mia sipped her coffee, listening intently and taking brief notes.

"Go on," she encouraged.

"So this Peter Steil goes under a different name, but has been keeping company with the count's daughter, Lana Safini. Lana has visited Mr. Steil in Grindelwald where he works for a helicopter company at the tourist bureau."

"What name does he go by and how can we be sure it's him?" she wanted to know, intrigued by the details provided so far.

"The alias he goes by in Italy is Peter Claasen, but there could be other names he uses. One of the security officers, Santo Mancini, placed a tracking device in the young aristocrat's cars, and also tailed her to a rendezvous in Grindelwald," he continued. Mia wrote down the address and description of the locations to be passed on to the American agents, whom she knew had arrived in Switzerland. Mia thanked Stefano, who promised to be in touch.

After ending the call, Mia relaxed back in the wooden chair to ponder her next move. Stefano had been informative, more than she expected. After a moment she placed a call. A younger woman with an American accent answered. Mia spoke clearly and succinctly. The woman at the other end of the line said nothing. After terminating the call, Mia walked out of the coffee shop and back to her office.

Chapter Thirty-five

Houston, Texas

Lilly Sands had just poured herself a cup of chamomile tea when the phone rang.

Hoping it was Mason, she rushed to answer it, almost dropping the receiver.

"Mason?" she asked hopefully. There was an uncomfortable silence.

"Mrs. Sands, this is Irma Trauber, the manager of the Kirbana Hotel," she said with discomfort in her tone.

"Oh!" Lilly exclaimed. "Have you located my husband?"

"I will need to pass you on to the police officer here. There has been an accident," Irma stated, her voice now trembling. A moment of silence followed.

"Hello, Mrs. Sands?" the officer enquired, with only a small hint of an accent.

"Yes," she replied, with a lump in her throat dreading what was coming next.

"I'm Detective Mann," he began as gently as he could. "I'm afraid to tell you that your husband has had an accident."

"What accident? What happened? Is he OK?" Lilly asked unbelievingly.

"Mrs. Sands, I'm very sorry, but your husband has passed away. It looks like he slipped in the shower and hit his head," Detective Mann said as kindly as he could manage.

"No! That can't be, there must be another explanation," Lilly argued. "There is no way he would be so clumsy."

The officer listened, then said, "We will do a postmortem examination to confirm the cause of death before signing a death certificate. Do you wish to have his belongings sent back—"

"I'm coming over there," Lilly interrupted. "I'm coming to take him home, so don't send anything yet. Do your autopsy because I think something else may have happened." She ended the call abruptly.

Lilly, still clutching the receiver, leaned against the wall. Her legs felt weak and she let them collapse under her, sliding to the floor. Her mouth was open but no sound came from it. She felt as if all the air had been sucked out of her lungs. Then, able to breathe again, she wailed like a wounded animal. The sound of deep sorrow enveloped her. Her soul ached.

On the other side of the world, Irma could only imagine what it would have been like to receive such a call. She sympathized with Mr. Sands' widow, unable to imagine how she would feel if anything happened to her beloved Otto.

Chapter Thirty-Six

Isabella, Grant and FBI agent Claudia Conti met in town for breakfast. The small bakery had a few tables and chairs where patrons could enjoy sweet snacks and a hot drink.

When Claudia entered the store, she quickly spotted her two colleagues tucking in to hot chocolate and apple strudel.

"Hi, Claudia. Come join us," Isabella, who was on her third piece of the strudel, said cheerfully.

"Yeah, please do," Grant chimed. "We don't want anything here going to waste. Although it seems unlikely with this one around. She's on her second breakfast!"

Claudia laughed as she pulled up a chair and helped herself to a cup of the chocolate drink. She smiled at them as they ate.

"Well?" Grant asked, wiping his sticky fingers on a napkin.

"Well, what?" Claudia teased.

"He wants to know if you've had contact from your contact," Isabella interjected, helping herself to the last piece of strudel.

"What contact?" the agent asked, enjoying keeping the two in suspense.

"You know, that lady from Interpol. Mia something or other," the mother-to-be said in a hushed voice, leaning in closer to her FBI friend.

"Ooh her!" Claudia said, feigning surprise. "Let me think." She frowned as if trying to recall details. "Umm…"

The suspense was just too much for Grant, who said with a serious tone, "Cut the nonsense, and let's have it." Both women looked at him, astonished by his reaction. Realizing this, his expression and voice softened when he spoke again.

"We don't have much time to work this, so please share."

Claudia explained that she was just teasing them and that she was well-known for this in her department back home. This level of mischief reminded Isabella of Marco, her twin brother, for whom she still grieved.

Sitting up straight and moving closer to her colleagues, Claudia quietly informed them of what Mia Strauss had told her.

"We have to trust the information and follow each lead," the agent stated.

Grant and Isabella nodded.

"I think one of us needs to stalk our man at the tourist bureau, get some photos," Isabella said, looking at Claudia as if assigning her this task.

"OK, I can do that, and you guys can get onto Google earth maps and orientate yourselves to the location of his cabin," Claudia suggested.

A plan was beginning to take shape. The trio agreed to meet for dinner for further consultation.

They left the little bakery separately. In a small town, one never knew who could be watching.

Chapter Thirty-Seven

Houston, Texas

Louis, Lilly's brother-in-law, leaned against his car, which he had parked in the driveway of his late brother-in-law's home. "Mason was a good man," Louis thought, reminiscing about the fishing trips they had enjoyed. Inside the modest house, a very determined Lilly was packing her suitcase while her sister Jane watched.

"Let me come with you," Jane said, concerned for her sister's emotional state.

"I'll be fine, stop worrying, Jane," Lilly answered. In frustration, she moved quickly from the closet to her suitcase on the bed and back to the closet again.

"It was probably just an accident. These things do happen," Jane said, trying to convince her sister, who apparently had convinced herself of foul play.

What Jane didn't know was the nature of the last conversation between Mason and his wife.

"Accidents don't happen to young, fit people," Lilly answered from the bathroom, where she was looking for her set of curlers.

"Uncle Al fell off the ladder and broke his hip, remember?" Jane argued back, hoping to calm her younger sister enough for her to concede and allow Jane to accompany her to Switzerland.

"Uncle Al was sixty-seven with no business being on that ladder in the first place, and you know it," her sister shot back.

Lilly closed her suitcase, picked up her handbag and moved past Jane toward the front door.

Lilly glanced around the house one last time and made sure the property was secure from unwanted intruders. Both women walked onto the porch, where Lilly fumbled with her keys before locking the front door. Louis placed the luggage in the trunk, which already contained a suitcase.

"What is this?" Lilly asked, surprised.

"I'm coming with you and that is that!" Jane replied, getting into the passenger seat.

Lilly looked at Louis, who just shrugged his broad shoulders, intimating that there was no point arguing about it further. He was right.

Chapter Thirty-Eight

Tourist Bureau, Grindelwald

Special Agent Claudia Conti followed the small narrow road out of town that led to the foot of the mountain. Here stood a small clubhouse, behind which she observed a large clearing for the helicopters to operate out of. Claudia had found the place easily following directions in a brochure she had obtained from the hotel concierge. She parked the rental car.

A helicopter came in for landing just before she got out of the car. She waited, observing six passengers alight from the aircraft as she readied her camera. She would have to reposition herself to get a better view and shot of the pilot. She did just that. Now, satisfied with the angle, she focused the long range lens on the pilot. Through the lens she could see it was indeed their man. He had removed his headset and was cleaning the lens of his sunglasses. She took several photos.

"Hey there, nice lady," a voice said flirtatiously. Claudia spun around to find another pilot leaning into her open car window and smiling at her. "You want to go for a flight?"

"Sure, but not today. I'm just getting some pictures of the Alps and beautiful scenery to send home," she replied, thinking quickly. He was still smiling at her but did not press her further.

"I hope to see you soon. The view from up there is even better," he said, pointing to the sky before walking away.

Claudia watched him join the other pilots and walk into the clubhouse.

Inside the clubhouse, Paul, the friendly pilot poured himself and other colleagues a cup of coffee. Sitting down next to Peter, he lit a cigarette.

"Who was that woman?" Peter asked him.

"Just a friendly tourist taking photos," Paul replied, blowing a plume of smoke toward the ceiling. "I think I drummed up some business. She may take a flight get more scenic photos to send back home."

"Where is home?" Peter pressed, feeling irritated at the thought of someone taking pictures.

"I think the US," Paul said, watching Peter who seemed perturbed by the information. "Don't worry, Mr. Casanova, she's definitively not your type. Plus I know you have another love interest," Paul winked. "I shall keep this one all to myself."

Both men laughed, but Peter didn't appreciate others knowing of his dalliances.

He had to be more careful.

Isabella and Grant had studied the satellite images on Google maps, locating Peter's cabin.

"Great. Let's get an idea of the surrounding area and best way to get closer," Grant said.

"You want to snoop around?" Isabella asked him.

"Yep, but let's meet with Claudia first to plan the next step," he replied, studying the thick forest surrounding the cabin and small dirt road leading to the porch. Isabella rested on the bed and closed her eyes. She was tired. It was time for a nap.

Chapter Thirty-Nine

Lilly Sands was exhausted by the time she reached the hotel in Zurich. The long trip coupled with the emotions of the last few days had taken their toll. The bellboy escorted the sisters up to their room, where Lilly collapsed onto the bed and began to sob. Jane sat next to her, holding her hand in an attempt to comfort her.

"Don't worry, sis," Jane said soothingly. "We'll get to the bottom of what happened and bring him home."

"You don't understand," Lilly sobbed. "I think I may be responsible for what happened."

"How do you mean?" Jane asked, curious to learn more.

"You know how I like to watch true crime shows." Jane nodded. "Well, I think I recognized someone on Americas Most Wanted from Mason's vacation photos and I told him. Being a journalist and anchor, he probably decided to look into it. Now he's dead and it's my fault." She began crying more desperately.

Jane didn't know what to think. There were two options, one being that there was some truth to this, even though she doubted it, and the second being that her sister was suffering from a psychotic break. Jane looked over at her sister, who had cried herself to sleep.

She didn't bother unpacking as tomorrow they would be flying to Bern, where they would board a train to the town of Grindelwald. The name of the place sent shivers down Jane's spine. She could hardly believe that only a few days ago she and Louis had considered booking a skiing trip there, after Mason had expressed such enthusiasm about the place. Not anymore.

Chapter Forty

Isabella and Claudia waited for Grant to return from an evening walk before setting off to dine at a local pub. The evening air was crisp with a light wind blowing down the mountain slope into the valley.

The pub was busy, allowing for greater anonymity. They ordered wiener schnitzel with potato salad and dumplings. Claudia and Grant drank beer, while Isabella ordered a Spezi, a non-alcoholic beverage of lemon iced tea and Coca Cola.

"I sure miss having a cheeseburger with fries," Isabella announced once the food had arrived.

"Don't be ungrateful," Grant replied. "This is all good, healthy food for the baby,'" he smiled and winked at her.

Isabella didn't respond. Now that a full plate of food was in front of her, she forgot all and tucked in the potato salad. Claudia and Grant watched for a brief moment as their very hungry companion maneuvered a large piece of schnitzel into her mouth.

"So, I went to the helicopter airfield today, and guess who I saw?" Claudia asked, cutting her meat and shoveling potato salad onto the fork. Grant wasn't in the mood for more guessing games, so answered, "Peter Steil".

"Correct!" said the FBI agent, smiling broadly.

"And?" Isabella asked, taking a moment to allow her food to travel down into her stomach.

"I have photos of him, but I think it would be a good idea if one of us went on a toured flight with him. Just to be sure," Claudia said thoughtfully, looking at her female colleague.

"Fine," Isabella replied, "but I still think we should get a closer look at that cabin he is hiding out in."

"One step at a time, Agatha Christie," Grant interjected, after taking a long swig of the delicious beer.

They decided to book a helicopter flight touring the famous the Eiger and Wetterhorn mountains. Grant agreed to call to find the schedule from the booking clerk, ensuring that they got onto the flight with their man.

"How are you going to manage that?" Isabella asked. "We can't be obvious by requesting a flight with a particular pilot. That will arouse suspicion and we don't want to spook him."

"Leave it to me, but you in the meantime can prepare your disguise for the trip," he said, imagining her wearing a Jackie O getup.

Claudia had brought up the photos taken that day at the airfield on her small laptop. The picture quality was excellent, and it was evident that the pilot was in fact Peter. Their Peter.

"It's settled then," Grant announced. "We do need more hard evidence that it's our guy, but thanks to the intel so far and with ongoing collaboration from our friends at the Bureau, it won't be long until we can move in and arrest him."

The trio got up to leave, but before they reached the exit, a familiar voice called out to Claudia. "Hey there, lovely lady, we meet again."

The agent's heart sank. "Oh no," she thought, as she hadn't disclosed the encounter with the young pilot. Turning, she saw Paul who beckoned for her to join him at the bar.

"I can't," she mouthed, and before he could protest, she was gone.

"Who was that?" Grant asked as they walked back to the hotel.

"One of the pilots I met today." That was all she was going to volunteer, fearing she may have already compromised the investigation. Nothing more was said about it. At least for now.

Chapter Forty-One

It had been a long day for Detective Mann of the Swiss police department, and it had left him rather tired. Sitting in his office, he stared at the autopsy report and accompanying photos of the late Mason Sands. The cause of death had not been blunt force trauma to the head, as he'd anticipated from the crime scene, but a fracture of the cervical spine. The man's neck had been broken—an injury that had to be inflicted by a strong and skilled pair of hands.

This was not an accidental death. Now Mann and his people were looking at a homicide. Mann sighed and rubbed his temples, before placing a call to the manager of the Kirbana Hotel, Mrs. Trauber.

"Good evening, detective," said a cheerful Irma. "What can I do for you at this hour?" she asked almost flirtatiously.

"Mrs. Trauber, I need your help," Mann answered seriously.

"Your wish is my command," Irma volunteered, curious at the request at this time of night.

"This conversation is confidential," the officer began, and continued once she had assured him that she could be trusted. "There has been a development in the case of Mr. Sands. I'm afraid to say that his suite is a crime scene and for now, needs to be treated as such. Nobody must enter other than the authorities."

Irma was silent, then spoke without mincing her words.

"My dear detective, that is impossible. The room has been cleaned from top to bottom by a team specialized for dealing with these situations," she explained. "It is our policy to have a forensic clean after a death in the hotel."

Mann thanked Irma, who before hanging up informed him that Mr. Sands' widow would be arriving the next day and had made a reservation in her hotel.

Mann thanked her again, then ended the call. "Damn! Damn!" he cursed under his breath. He had a real problem. A homicide, a clean crime scene, not a shred of evidence, a murderer on the loose, and if that wasn't enough, a bereaved widow who would want answers.

It was time to call it a night. Collecting the reports lying before him, he placed them in a filing cabinet, which he then locked. He felt defeated.

On his way home, Mann walked past the small town church and stopped in front of it. Reaching for the door, he was surprised to find it still open. Mann entered the Baroque-style edifice, knelt in front of the cross supporting a figure of Christ, and began to pray. He prayed for a miracle.

Irma walked out of her small office lost in thought. She felt unsettled by the conversation she had just had with the detective. A murder in her hotel was unimaginable. As she crossed the foyer, she heard a woman call to her with a southern American drawl.

"Excuse me, Ma'am."

Irma looked over to find two ladies in their forties standing at the front desk.

"Good evening," Irma greeted them with a broad smile as she walked toward them. "Can I help you?"

"Yes, you can. I'm Lilly Sands and this is my sister. We have a reservation and would like to check in."

Irma welcomed the pair and efficiently helped them settle into their room. The impression the widow gave was that of a person who was bereaved but also determined to find out what happened to her late husband. "This is a no nonsense lady," Irma thought. The next few days would be interesting.

Chapter Forty-Two

Isabella woke early and decided to go for a brisk walk before breakfast. She missed her husband Nick, who had always been supportive of her ambitions. They had been talking most days by e-mail, interspersed by an occasional brief phone call. The difference in time zones made the latter more difficult.

Today was going to be important. It had been decided that she and Grant would go on a helicopter ride. For the first time in months, she would be faced with the fugitive. Her disguise would be simple, consisting of a wig of short brown hair, Jackie O sunglasses and a killer smile.

The most important part of her persona would be to be mute. The scenario Grant had concocted in order to secure a flight with Peter Steil when making the booking was that his wife had undergone throat surgery, and this was a surprise trip for her bravery. Post-op recovery forbid her from speaking, hence having a pilot fluent in English would make it easier to understand descriptions of the views without needing to ask questions. The booking clerk bought it.

At ten that morning, they would be at the airfield. Isabella had mixed feelings about seeing a man she had met in LA who had been so charming. It was hard to believe that she had been attracted to a wanted killer.

Isabella walked into the breakfast room where she spotted Special Agent Claudia Conti sitting alone at a table adjacent to the window. The agent had a strange expression, as if concentrating intensely on a conversation. Isabella noticed two women were sitting at the neighboring table. They were American and engrossed in a private discussion. The slimmer lady was visibly upset, speaking louder than her companion wanted, requiring frequent reminding to lower her voice.

Claudia caught Isabella's eye as she walked past her, heading toward the very inviting breakfast buffet.

Isabella was famished. Everything in front of her looked so delicious, making the food difficult to resist. With her breakfast neatly piled onto a large plate, she made her way to sit opposite Claudia, but at a different table.

"If they think they can brush me off, they have something coming," Isabella heard one of the Americans state forcefully, with the other replying, "Let's just wait and see what they tell us first, sis. There's no use getting all worked up just yet."

Isabella looked at her colleague with a raised eyebrow. The agent acknowledged her by responding with a wink.

The two women finished their bacon, sausage and eggs and left the dining area. Lilly was on a mission, starting at the Grindelwald Police Station. Detective Mann was definitely going to need the miracle he had prayed for a few hours earlier.

Chapter Forty-Three

Grant, Isabella and Claudia drove in the rental Range Rover to the airfield. During the journey they learned from Claudia about the two women at breakfast discussing meeting with the police. One of the ladies' husband had been found dead in his suite at their hotel. It made Isabella think of the strange smell on arrival.

"The widow was adamant that her husband had met with foul play, but the police had ruled it an accident," Claudia informed them.

"Maybe we can help," Grant remarked.

"We have other things to focus on," Isabella said firmly. She had not come here to get involved in matters that weren't of their concern.

"Here we are," Claudia announced, parking the car in a large bay at the edge of the parking lot.

With Claudia a little ahead of the others, the trio made their way to the small office, where they were met by a friendly member of the ground staff.

Isabella was wearing her disguise. Through the window she could see a pilot assisting passengers into a helicopter.

Once the formalities of checking in were completed, another pilot approached them to escort them to the waiting chopper.

"Lovely lady!" an enthusiastic voice said. Claudia turned around to find Paul, the friendly pilot she had met days earlier while doing reconnaissance for the mission, smiling at her. "Oh boy," she thought, but still smiled back at him.

"You, my dear, are flying in my bird, yes?" he said, taking her gently by the arm and escorting her to his chopper. Claudia had no choice. If she protested it would be considered rude and arouse suspicion.

As Isabella and Grant watched on anxiously, a man approached them. It was Peter Steil.

"Welcome!" he said confidently, wearing a broad smile. "My name is Peter Claasen and I'll be your pilot today." Isabella recognized him instantly. In spite of the hair style, neatly trimmed beard, and colored contacts he was wearing, she never forgot a person's facial expression or voice.

Suddenly she felt nauseated, but chose to go ahead with the planned flight. At least she could tell her partners with confidence that this pilot was certainly their man.

"What's your name, sweetheart?" Peter asked Isabella, who remained quiet.

"She's my wife, Mrs. Simms," Grant answered for her, playing the role of the protective husband.

"Can't she answer a question herself, buddy?" Peter retorted, displaying arrogance.

"Normally she's quite a chatter box, but she's had throat surgery recently, so doctor's orders are resting the vocal chords," Grant answered back. Peter snorted, then led the couple to the chopper and helped Isabella into the front seat next to his, directing Grant to sit with the others in the back.

"Better view at the front," Peter whispered into Isabella's ear, and then he looked back at Grant and smirked.

The rotors started turning, generating thrust for the gentle and controlled lift off. Peter steered the aircraft onto a northeasterly heading before climbing to the allocated altitude.

They followed the chopper piloted by Paul, who was now happily in the company of Special Agent Claudia Conti. They passed prairies, glaciers and the famous mountains. Peter found a nice location on the east side of the mountain to hover while his passengers took photos. He was surprised that the lady sitting next to him was not as interested in the scenic view as others. He kept the helicopter in the hover configuration while he studied Isabella. There was something familiar about her, but he couldn't place her. In truth, there had been many willing women in his life, but this lady stood out for some reason. He wasn't convinced by the throat surgery story—the woman looked strong, not sickly. This unnerved him. He needed to get a reaction from her.

He came up with a plan.

"Tango, Alpha, Oscar, we are returning to base," Peter announced through his headset to his fellow pilot Paul in the other chopper.

"Roger, see you back there," Paul replied.

With that, Peter maneuvered his aircraft into a steep climbing turn, before pitching the nose down to return to a straight and level flight path. He noted that the maneuver frightened his passenger and she had almost cried out. He decided to push the aircraft to its structural limit of flight, by a series of almost aerobatic routines. Peter noticed that other passengers appeared thrilled with the ride, but not this lady. Isabella gripped the armrest firmly, making her knuckles blanch. Isabella could feel the bile travel up her throat and into her mouth. No longer able to contain sound or the contents of her stomach, she vomited all over the control panel.

Peter was not impressed. The aerobatics stopped abruptly. He made no effort to reach for a sick bag or open the air vents for her benefit. He had heard a profanity she had uttered under her breath.

Other passengers, including Grant, gave Isabella handkerchiefs and paper towels to help her clean herself up. She thanked them with a nod, but made no effort to wipe down the instrument panel. As far as she was concerned, the flight was over.

Chapter Forty-Four

Grindelwald Police Station was a modest two-story building with modern trimmings and courteous staff. Detective Mann was at his desk when his secretary announced that he had visitors.

"Who?" he demanded to know. When she informed him that it was Mrs. Sands, his heart sank.

"Bring her in," he said, not expecting Mrs. Sands to be accompanied by her sister.

"I'm Detective Mann," he began, inviting them to sit after shaking hands. "I'm so sorry that we are not meeting under better circumstances," he said empathically.

"I know who you are," Lilly Sands replied somewhat impatiently. "I couldn't imagine any other circumstances we'd be meeting in. Can you?"

He couldn't. The lady before him was not going to be easy to handle.

"Would you like a cup of coffee?" he offered, hoping to buy some time before taking on what would be a trying meeting.

"No, thank you, but I want to understand what happened to my husband."

Mann informed her of what he knew, including the autopsy report. He could not hide this from her.

"I've visited my husband in the morgue this morning, so you can appreciate that this is a lot for me to take in. Please bring me his personal effects and maybe we can find a clue," Lilly said calmly.

The detective called his assistant, requesting the box of the deceased's belongings be brought to his office. While they waited, Lilly told him about her last conversation with her husband and her suspicions of a certain helicopter pilot being a wanted man in the US.

Mann listened and took notes.

"We don't have any fingerprints, DNA or fibers that can help us," he stated sadly. "So how are we going to prove anything?"

"Detective," Lilly began, now more gentle in her approach "I can see that you are a good man and that this is not easy for you either, but take a look at these images." Lilly produced a thumb drive and leaned over the desk to plug it into the detective's computer. The image of Peter Steil from the TV show came up, then she displayed the photo of the helicopter pilot taken by her Mason.

"I cannot see much of a resemblance," Mann stated, looking at the images.

There was a knock at the door. A young female officer entered with a suitcase and a box of other minor items. Mann thanked his colleague. Together, Lilly and her sister went through the belongings, ticking each item off the list placed in front of them. The detective stood aside watching.

"There's something missing," Lilly said suddenly.

"Oh? What?" Mann asked, doubting it would be anything of importance.

"His laptop. His phone is here but the battery is flat," the widow observed.

"What kind of laptop is it?" the detective asked.

"An Apple with his name engraved on the side," she answered. "Find it and you've got your killer!"

The detective considered his options, which weren't many. Lilly Sands had become his ally, and perhaps there was some truth to her theory. He decided to look into the pilot in question.

Lilly and her sister left the police station feeling a little more hopeful that the truth would come out in one way or another.

"Can you imagine if we help solve this and get to tell our story on one of those famous crime shows you like?" Jane remarked. Her sister didn't appreciate this misplaced enthusiasm and in no uncertain terms let her know. So together they walked through the town center, pondering what else they could do to help the seemingly pessimistic detective.

Chapter Forty-Five

Villa Safini, Milan

Lana Safini had just returned from the stables after a long ride on her favorite horse, Felix, when her phone rang.

"*Pronto?*" she answered in Italian, oblivious to her phone being tapped.

"*Ciao, bellissima!*" a voice greeted her.

"Peter!" she exclaimed, happy to hear from him. "I've missed you so much," she said sincerely.

"Me too, my love, which is why I'm calling," he explained. "I wanted to see you again, so I was planning on flying to Milan this afternoon for a couple of days."

"Please come and stay here, we'll have such fun!" Lana promised.

"Fantastic! My plane arrives at ten tonight. See you soon," he said as sincerely as he could muster. He ended the call after confirming that a car would be sent to pick him up.

Peter had felt unsettled after the incident involving the mysterious woman earlier that day. He hated the feeling of not being in control, which is why he needed to distance himself from his work for a few days. Lana would be the perfect distraction. Paul had agreed to fill in for him and to keep an eye on his cabin while he was away.

Peter felt better now that he had secured a plan for the next few days. He was sure that when he returned, there would be a new turnover of tourists. He could to put the whole incident behind him.

Chapter Forty-Six

Claudia was in her small hotel room cleaning her gun when there was a gentle knock at the door.

"Who is it?" she called out.

"It's us," Isabella replied.

Claudia let them in and continued cleaning her gun. Isabella was eating an apple so she let Grant do the talking.

"Have you heard anything from Interpol?" he asked, hoping that the next stage of their plan could be implemented without delay.

"Not yet, but—" She was interrupted by her cell beeping. She answered, putting the phone on speaker.

"Hello?"

"It's Mia Strauss," the caller announced, and before Claudia could respond, went on to say, "I've been informed from Italy that the man has traveled to Milan this afternoon and is visiting Countess Lana Safini."

"How do you know he is residing at her villa?" Claudia asked.

"Our informant, Santo, confirmed it," Mia said.

Claudia thanked the Swiss agent for keeping them abreast, and briefly outlined their next move.

Operation 'cabin search' had been launched.

Chapter Forty-Seven

The cabin's remoteness, with its lush forest surrounding it, would have been difficult to detect from the small dirt track leading up to it. A large trunk from a fallen tree shielded the man from view, giving him the perfect spot from which to observe any activity at the cabin.

A car with three occupants approached, stopping in front of the small wooden building. The man sank back into his hiding spot, picked up his binoculars and focused them for a clearer view. Two women and a man got out of the car, walked up the porch and peered through the windows before going around to the rear of the cabin. Not recognizing the visitors, he considered his options. He decided to wait.

Grant had managed to pick the lock of the back door, and gently pushed it open. He waited and listened. It was dead quiet. Feeling comfortable that they were alone, the agents entered the premises. They spread, out moving quickly and quietly into the sparsely furnished rooms.

Isabella looked for hidden panels in the walls and floorboards, where a hidden stash of documents and the like could be kept. She found nothing. Moving into the bathroom, she examined the medicine cabinet. Its dimensions seemed odd when she considered the amount of contents it should have been able to hold. Removing the few items from within, she tapped on its posterior wall and found a false partition.

"I've found something!" she called out to the others, who joined her in the cramped bathroom.

Behind the partition hid a small safe with a touch screen keypad.

"How do you suppose we get this thing open? We can't just smash it," Grant commented.

Isabella picked up a bottle of talcum powder she had removed from the cabinet and held it up for Grant to see.

"With that?" he questioned, baffled.

Isabella sprinkled the white powder onto the keypad and blew away any excess.

"Our hands leave oils and amino acids on the surfaces we touch, which allows the powder to stick," she explained. Claudia stepped forward to study the panel. The main keys that had been used were only three, allowing her to find the combination without much effort. She opened its small door, reached inside and pulled out its contents.

"We have some Euro, documents with social security numbers, passports," she said, handing the latter to Isabella.

"Well, well!" she exclaimed. "We have one for a Peter Steil, a Peter Brooks and a Patrick Steil," she announced, reminding the others that Patrick had been Peter's twin brother whom he'd killed.

"I presume he has the Peter Claasen passport with him, since he's gone to Italy," Grant concluded.

"OK, let's take these as evidence," Claudia said, opening a small transparent bag for Isabella to place the documents into after she'd finished wiping the sink of excess talcum powder.

"Give me a moment to use the restroom," Isabella said, locking the door for privacy.

Grant and Claudia stood in the narrow hallway. While they waited for her, they chatted about some of their experiences as young police officers involving bank heists.

The man hiding outside grew restless and curious as to the activities within the cabin. After satisfying himself that he wasn't spotted, he snuck up to the side of the cabin. Through the window he could see two figures standing in the hallway. After moving to the open door at the rear, he stopped to draw his weapon. Slowly and quietly, he followed the sound of the voices, and approached with caution. Grant had not heard the man creep up behind him. His presence only now became apparent by the cold steel barrel Grant felt pressed up against the nape of his neck. Claudia stood as if frozen on the spot.

Isabella was drying her hands when she became aware of the eerie silence in the hallway. Pressing her ear to the bathroom door, she strained to listen.

"Who are you people and what are you doing here?" the man demanded to know.

"We could ask you the same," Claudia replied. The man held his gun aimed at Grant's neck. He moved toward the female agent and snatched the evidence bag from her. Still keeping an eye on the two strangers, he studied its contents.

"We're FBI," Claudia volunteered, "and you?"

The man stood still, studying them, before saying, "Sure you are, and I'm Elvis."

Claudia produced her ID and opened it, moving forward slightly so that the man could confirm her prior statement. He sighed, allowing the arm holding his gun to drop and replacing the weapon in its holster.

The tension in the air dissipated almost immediately.

"OK, I guess we're on the same side. I'm Detective Mann from Grindelwald police precinct," he said, relieved that there wouldn't be a showdown.

The bathroom door opened and Isabella emerged. Grant introduced her to the Swiss officer.

The group exchanged information providing a rationale for their interest in Peter Steil aka Claasen. The trio learned that their fugitive was also a possible suspect in the murder of Mason Sands and that his widow was in town with her sister demanding answers.

"Remember the two ladies I was eavesdropping on?" Claudia asked her colleagues, but Isabella appeared distracted. Something had caught her eye.

"You OK?" Grant asked, concerned. She ignored him and proceeded to walk toward the bookshelf, where she lifted a messy pile of magazines to expose a badly hidden piece of technology.

Mann hurried toward her, picked it up, and turned it over. It was engraved with a name: Mason Sands.

"This belonged to the murder victim," Mann informed the group. "I'll take it back to our lab for examination and finger printing."

Isabella informed her Swiss colleague that they would proceed with their own plan, but would keep him updated on their progress. They exchanged phone numbers before going their separate ways.

Detective Mann's prayers had been answered in more ways than one.

Chapter Forty-Eight

Lilly and Jane were preparing for a quiet night in when the phone rang. Jane, who was closest to it, answered.

"Hello?" After a brief pause, she said, "It's for you," and handed the receiver to Lilly, who was setting her hair with curlers.

"Yes, this is she," she stated. "You have? That is wonderful!" she exclaimed, before ending the call. Turning to her sister, she said, "I think we can celebrate." Lilly informed her that Detective Mann had a solid lead in the case. "Time for some nice room service and a bottle of champagne," she said browsing through the restaurant's menu. Jane shared her sister's enthusiasm, hoping it would not be short-lived.

Suddenly there was a knock at their door. The sisters looked at each other before Lilly got up to look through the peephole.

"It's that woman from the dining room," Lilly said. She unlatched the chain, allowing the door to be opened by a few centimeters. She looked at the badge held up for her to read more clearly. FBI Special Agent Claudia Conti.

"There must be some mistake," Jane remarked from behind her sister, who had let the agent into the room. The agent gave away as much information as she could, mainly warning the two women that they could be in danger. Strategies to keep safe were discussed briefly. Then Conti left. The sisters' beacon of hope for justice had been dimmed by a more sinister threat.

Peter Steil.

Chapter Forty-Nine

It was a warm spring night in the Milanese hills. The dark sky was littered with bright stars and the moon radiated a soft light over the fields, creating a picturesque view from Lana's private balcony.

Santo's day had been filled with chaperoning Lana and her male companion, to a local winery, where they spent the day enjoying the luxuries of privileged life. Carefree, Lana drove her Alfa Romeo Spider through the winding country roads. Peter sat in the passenger seat, his arm resting gently on the convertible's door frame, his hand placed on its exterior and fingers tapping to the music from the car stereo. This gave Santo an idea.

It was late at night and all was still on the grounds of the villa. Santo made his way to the garage where the car had been parked, and positioned himself to conceal his activities around the passenger door. He would have to work quickly, not having the benefit of technology, but he didn't mind being old school. He placed the kit on the ground, lit his small torch and shone the beam onto the area of interest. He dusted the print with a fiber brush holding adhesive powder, lifted it with special tape, and sealed it for preservation of its integrity.

He felt satisfied.

The tranquility was interrupted by footsteps hurrying across the gravel path leading to the garage. Santo sank back into the shadows behind the sports car and listened. A man's voice uttered a profanity before getting into the Safini limousine, slamming its door and backing out of the parking space.

Santo edged toward the garage door to see the car parked up at the main entrance. The chauffeur stepped out and opened the rear passenger door. Santo could see two figures standing at the foot of the steps. Lana was kissing her lover good bye.

Peter was leaving. Santo had to act quickly. He ran to the cottage he shared with colleague and friend Patrizio.

"Get that Interpol agent Stefano on the phone!" he said, almost commanding. "Tell him to expect an e-mail with an attachment of a hand print of the wanted man."

Patrizio did as was requested, while Santo scanned the print and uploaded it onto the computer ready to send the message.

"I've got him on the line. Anything else you want me to convey?" Patrizio asked.

"Yeah, tell him that Peter has left the villa and is likely to be headed back to Grindelwald," Santo replied.

"How do you know that?" Patrizio asked.

"Because I've tapped her car, phone and room to overhear their conversations."

Agent Stefano confirmed receiving the e-mail, which he would be forwarding to his contact in Switzerland, Mia

Strauss. She in turn would alert the trio from the States and other relevant authorities. The net around the hunted was tightening.

Isabella's cell phone rang, rousing her from a deep sleep. Sitting up in bed and looking at the screen she could see it was Mia.

"Hello?" she answered, still drowsy.

"I'm forwarding you an e-mail with an attachment of your man's prints," she said, and without wasting time filled Isabella in on how they had been obtained and Peter's imminent return to Switzerland. Isabella thanked her and hung up.

"Who was that?" Grant, now also awake, asked from the sofa where he had been sleeping. He moved closer to watch as Isabella opened the e-mail and its attachment, and stared at the screen in awe.

"That's a great print and piece of evidence," he remarked.

"It is indeed. Now I just need to alert Detective Mann on what Mia has just told me," she concluded, proceeding to forward the e-mail to the Swiss officer and also to her boss, Chief Paoli, with whom she had remained in regular communication.

The two detectives were startled when the phone rang. It was Detective Mann.

"I got your message," he said, sounding under the weather.

"You still awake?" Grant asked. They had him on speakerphone to facilitate a three-way conversation.

"Yes, and I'm enjoying a bottle of Schnapps." Grant and Isabella exchanged glances, worried at what was coming next.

"The laptop has been wiped down. So no fingerprints. Nothing!" Mann almost shouted.

Grant spoke with an even tone, making plans to arrest Peter the next morning. It was decided that it would be too risky to apprehend him at the cabin; the safer alternative would be the airfield at the start of his shift. They agreed to meet there. They had a warrant for his arrest and he could be taken into custody under suspicion of murdering Mason Sands.

They had a viable plan. Isabella climbed back into bed, but before Grant could switch off the lights, her phone rang again. It was Chief Paoli.

"Good news!" he announced. "I've received confirmation that the print you sent is a positive match to that on file in his marine records and to those on the gun that killed the Steil parents. Good work!"

Isabella and Grant finally got a good night's sleep. The pace of the hunt had just begun to quicken.

Chapter Fifty

Grindelwald, 05:00

Peter opened the door to his cabin, relieved to be home and alone again. He would only be graced with three hours sleep before having to get ready for a day of flying.

He threw his bag onto his bed, stripped off while walking to the bathroom and enjoyed a warm shower. After drying off, he wrapped the towel around his waist and looked at himself in the mirror. He looked tired. To ease the stiffness in his neck, he stretched and moved his head from side to side. Suddenly he stopped and looked at the toilet. Its seat was in the 'up' position. He never left the seat up; it was something his mother had punished him for as a child.

Peter took a step back from the basin and slowly looked around the small bathroom. Underneath the sink he spied a small trace of white powder. Kneeling, he touched it and smelled it. It was talcum powder. Peter stood up abruptly and swung open the cabinet door. The items had been moved. The tension in his body that had eased with the warm water returned. He tore open the false partition hiding the small safe and punched in the code with urgency. He stared at the remaining contents. The passports were gone. He still had the one he had traveled to Italy on.

Someone had invaded his space. Peter made a choice not to wait around to find out who that might have been. He would leave town before dawn. Nobody was going to catch him. He had found freedom and was determined to keep it. He was prepared to kill for it if he had to.

Chapter Fifty-One

The airfield was busy with the first tourists of the day. Grant, Detective Mann, Isabella and Claudia had been staking out the area for an hour before the first flights were due to depart.

There was no sign of Peter. Claudia spotted her friendly pilot, Paul, and approached him.

"Hi there, Paul," she said enthusiastically, waving as she walked toward him.

"Why, hello, my lovely lady," he greeted back. "Keen for another flight?" he asked hopefully.

"No, I'm afraid, my friends and I have other plans," she explained.

"Oh, so what brings you here?" he asked, now curious but hoping that he would be able to ask her out to dinner.

"My friend was sick in the helicopter the other day and wanted to apologize to the pilot," she said, sounding sincere.

"Peter Claasen, you mean. Well, he was due to come back to work today but nobody has seen him. He went on a naughty weekend if you know what I mean," Paul volunteered, winking at her.

Claudia thanked him and returned to join her colleagues.

"He's gone," she informed them, still smiling and waving at Paul who was getting into an aircraft.

"We have to think of a plan B," Isabella said. The foursome decided to return to the police precinct to formulate it. The fugitive was once again in the wind.

Chapter Fifty-Two

Detective Mann's office was spacious, furnished with good modern taste, and overlooked the Grindelwald train station. The detective and his fellow foreign colleagues sat around an oval tabl that supported a computer, various case files and, what Isabella appreciated most, a healthy assortment of Swiss snacks.

Agent Conti had requested a teleconference with the Interpol agents and American and Italian authorities to discuss the recent events and progress the mission.

"He's disappeared, and is presumably traveling under the name Peter Claasen, since we've confiscated all the other passports," Isabella said.

"Do we know where he might have gone?" Chief of Interpol asked.

"He could be anywhere, but I'd bet he would look to get assistance from friends with benefits," Mia Strauss concluded.

"You mean he could go back to see his little friend Lana Safini?" Stefano asked.

"It's a possibility," Grant conceded. "Who is the contact in the Safini household, Stefano?"

"His name is Santo Mancini. He is very smart and has been able to provide crucial information about our man's movements by using tracking and listening devices. And he got us those prints."

"Contact him, inform him of what we know and get him to liaise with me directly if Peter shows up again," Isabella ordered. The group looked at her, not knowing what to make of her change in demeanor. She spoke with authority, but obviously hadn't read the body language of others present. An uncomfortable, deafening silence followed.

"Good idea," Grant said eventually, hoping to dissipate the strangeness of the atmosphere. "For now, we'll sit tight and ask our colleagues of the Swiss and Italian police departments to be ready to intervene."

The meeting came to an end, leaving Isabella with renewed determination. Soon they would catch him and she was prepared to pull the trigger.

There was a knock at the door, but before Mann could respond, it swung open and in charged Lilly Sands with her sister in tow. The four officers stared at them dumbfounded. A very apologetic secretary entered the office, but Detective Mann reassured her that he would handle the situation. After she had left, he demanded an explanation for the intrusion.

"We're frightened," Lilly blurted, then recognizing the FBI agent, pointed at her and added, "She said we were in danger."

"I said that it may be a possibility, but we talked about strategies to keep you safe," Claudia clarified.

"We want protection and we want it now!" Lilly demanded.

The two sisters stood in the office, arms folded, refusing to leave until an officer had been assigned for their protection. Detective Mann called for his secretary, asking her to summon Officer Schultz, who arrived minutes after. Armed with information and his newly assigned task, he introduced himself to the sisters and offered to escort them back to the hotel. Thanking Mann, they left, contented with the arrangement.

Isabella and her two colleagues soon after returned to the hotel, where Isabella took another much needed nap.

Chapter Fifty-Three

Malpensa International Airport, Milan

Peter had been furious when he left his cabin in a hurry before dawn that morning. He had driven to Bern, where he boarded a plane to Milan. He felt hunted, but not trapped quite yet. He considered his options carefully during the drive to Bern. When he arrived at the airport, before boarding the plane, he booked a small charter flight from Milan to Lake Como.

Upon arriving in Milan, he had time to spare before the connecting flight. After clearing customs, Peter made his way to the men's room. He shaved, trimmed his hair with clippers and replaced the contact lenses with thin rimmed spectacles.

The door to the public bathroom opened. A young cleaner pushing a mop and pail entered and began cleaning the floor. Peter smiled at him, leaving a generous tip on the small plate at the entrance. The youth turned to thank him, but Peter was already on the move.

Lake Como was a popular holiday destination for the rich and famous. Hollywood stars had bought property with gorgeous views of the famous lake. Peter had booked a deluxe room at the Hotel il Sereno, which faced the lake with the mountains as a backdrop. Ironically, the name of this hotel translated into English to mean "the serene". Peter was anything but serene.

Chapter Fifty-Four

Lake Como, Northern Italy

Peter decided not to unpack his small suitcase, hoping that his stay would be brief. After showering, he sat on the edge of the large bed and called the one person he could depend on and who in turn was emotionally dependent on him. Countess Lana Safini.

As he waited for her to pick up, he went through the next stage of his escape.

"*Pronto?*" she answered.

"Lana, *amore*, how are you?" he said sounding as enthusiastic as she was likely to be.

"Peter? Where are you? I thought you were back at work," she said in surprise.

"There's been a slight change of plan. I reconsidered the invitation to your grandmother's ninetieth birthday. It would be impolite of me not to attend after the hospitality and generosity your family has shown me," he fawned.

"Where are you now?" she wanted to know.

"A beautiful place, my love. Lake Como." He hoped she would send a private helicopter to pick him up.

"The party is tomorrow night here at the villa," she said. "How quickly can you get here? There are so many things to prepare," Lana went on. "Although thankfully I don't have to do much other than look gorgeous and attend." She giggled.

Peter rolled his eyes then replied. "I'm sure I could be with you very soon if you have your father's private chopper fly me over."

"Absolutely!" she exclaimed. "I shall tell Papa at once."

Arrangements were made for him to be picked up first thing the next morning. All he needed was a good night's sleep, and tomorrow would take care of itself.

Santo had overheard the whole exchange between Lana and her lover. Wasting no time, he contacted Stefano from Interpol with the itinerary of the grand birthday celebration.

Stefano, as promised, contacted Isabella and her crew directly with the update. After thanking him, she requested another teleconference to set a trap. This time the Italian police and other agents who had experience with undercover operations were involved in strategizing the plan. This included their inside man, Santo.

That evening Isabella and her crew boarded a plane for Milan. The net was closing. Soon she would have her fugitive in handcuffs.

Chapter Fifty-Five

Villa Safini, 10:00

Lana was looking forward to taking Peter shopping since he had no formal evening wear. Milan, the capital of the fashion world, had much to offer a well-built young man who was being doted on by a wealthy aristocrat. They found casual and evening wear at Louis Vuitton.

"You look so handsome," she purred as he admired himself in the mirror of the dressing room.

He smiled at her but said nothing. Their next stop was to buy a pair of dark dress shoes. Lana was excited he would be at her side that evening. She had something she wanted to share with him, but it would have to wait.

Piling the boxes of merchandize into the trunk of her BMW, he suggested a quick snack at a local bar. Lana agreed. They sat outside a small eatery adjacent to the famous opera house, enjoying a classic Italian sandwich and iced coffee.

Being a weekend, at that time of day the traffic was not that heavy. Oblivious to anything else going on around them, neither noticed the black Mercedes drive past with three passengers inside. One of them peered out of her window and saw him. They too had gone on a shopping spree for the evening's festivities.

Much as she wanted to stop the car and detain him then and there, she resisted. For now, she would have to be patient.

Santo, Patrizio and Stefano met with other agents in the small cottage at the rear of the property to go over some of the finer details of Operation Fugitive.

Luigi was a well-seasoned undercover agent who had orchestrated additional police officers to play a role in the sting. They would pose as security and catering staff.

Grant and Special Agent Claudia Conti would be present as 'invited guests'. Falsification of an invitation had been arranged by Santo and Patrizio. They were to pose as Sir James Grant and Lady Claudia.

The wheels had been set in motion. It was only a matter of hours before the tables turned on Peter Steil.

Chapter Fifty-Six

Grand Hotel, Milan

"Why can't I participate?" Isabella demanded to know. She was furious with Grant who had decided not to include her in the undercover operation.

"I've rented a dress, shoes, make up," she pleaded, unable to believe what she was hearing. Taking the invitations Santo had provided, she waved them at Grant, who had grown increasingly concerned for his colleague's emotional state. She had shown signs of emotional lability and impulsivity, which he was told by a visiting doctor at the hotel in Grindelwald was considered quite normal in a gravid lady.

He was getting dressed for the evening when there was a knock at the door. Isabella opened it, letting Claudia into the suite. The younger female agent looked stunning in the Versace-like evening gown.

"Can you believe this?" she shrieked at the FBI agent, who realized that Grant was out of his depth at dealing with a fuming Isabella.

"Hey, hey, come here," Claudia said soothingly, taking over from Grant, who had disappeared into the bathroom.

"I know that this is tough and unfair after all the work you've put into this case," she began, "but you've got to understand that we've promised your husband and Chief Paoli that we'd take care of you and not place you or the baby in the line of fire."

"I recognize him, I can catch him," Isabella insisted. "What if he eludes you? I've put my personal life on hold for this."

"Exactly. This is why we don't want you getting hurt, so that in future you can enjoy family life," Claudia said emphasizing the word 'family'.

Isabella sat on the edge of the bed pouting like a five-year-old who wasn't allowed to have ice cream. Claudia sat next to her and placed her arm around her. Isabella rested her head on her shoulder, sighing deeply.

"If it makes you feel any better, on the trip home, I'll upgrade you to business class," she promised.

"On your lousy salary?" the mother-to-be asked with a laugh.

"I've got some savings, and if it means keeping you out of harm's way, then it'll be worth every penny," she answered sincerely. "Plus you get all-you-can-eat buffet at all hours of each of the time zones."

That did appeal to Isabella. She smiled at Claudia and agreed to play along.

"You can come out of hiding," Claudia called out to Grant, who hesitantly emerged from the bathroom looking smart in his suit. The concierge rang the room, letting the couple know that the limousine had arrived and was waiting. The two agents checked that their earpieces and microphones were in place before bidding farewell to a still-grumpy Isabella.

Chapter Fifty-Seven

Lana and Peter were dressed and ready to join the Safini family down stairs, but the young countess had other plans. Taking Peter by the hand, she led him into her large suite. Enamored, she looked up at him and smiled.

"What is it?" he asked, his curiosity piqued by the hints she had dropped that afternoon about a surprise.

"I was going to tell you sooner, but I thought tonight would be the best occasion, in light of a grand celebration of life," she said, barely containing her excitement.

"Go on," he encouraged, feeling a pit developing in his stomach.

"I'm pregnant!" Lana took his hands and drew him closer to her.

"What?! Are you sure? How far along?" he asked, thinking of how he might convince her to terminate it.

"Early days, four weeks the doctor told me," she said. "Isn't this wonderful? We can start a family and have our wedding here," she gushed, but Peter had stopped listening. To hide his rage, he drew her to him as if to hug her. Lana misread the force of this embrace. He was furious. This was not the plan. This was not *his* plan.

Finally he let her go and with his usual suave charm, led her to believe that all was well.

"Wait for me downstairs," he told her. "I'll join you in a few minutes." Before she left, he made her promise to keep this their secret for the time being. In love and excited, Lana promised.

Peter returned to his suite, locked the door and with clenched fists paced around the room like an animal in captivity. He breathed heavily, his nostrils flaring; he was seething with rage. He wanted to hurt himself like he had as a youth to deal with extreme stress. Storming into the bathroom, he took a hand towel, folded it into a mouth guard, placed it between his teeth and bit down as hard as he could.

It relieved some of the tension. He felt better and more able to formulate a plan. Glancing out his window, he could see the first guests arriving. He checked his watch. The party was about to begin. He would play the part of the perfect boyfriend, dispose of her and then disappear. Forever.

Back at the Grand Hotel, Isabella was getting restless. Unable to take her mind off the mission, she opened her wardrobe and placed the evening dress on the bed. Looking in the mirror, she played with her hair, putting it up, then letting it drop. She wouldn't need much make up, having been blessed with tanned skin and, courtesy of her hormonal status, with a glowing complexion. She opened the drawer and took out the earpiece and her weapon. In spite of not having an invitation, she would improvise to gain access to the party.

Isabella was not going to be stopped. Tonight, she would be doing the stopping.

Chapter Fifty-Eight

Villa Safini

The villa was exquisitely decorated. Lilies, roses and chrysanthemums filled the air with an exotic aroma. The long table in the dining room was set immaculately, with a pressed white linen table cloth, matching napkins and highly polished silverware. The Waterford crystal glassware sparkled, enhancing the crisp color of the champagne it held.

Count Safini had promised his mother that he had a big surprise in store for her later in the evening. The elderly lady was looking forward to it. They were joined by Lana and Peter, who were a seemingly happy and handsome couple. More guests arrived, leading the Safini family to mingle and enjoy the festivities.

Santo stood at the entrance checking invitations, while his friend Patrizio lingered around the main stairwell. Grant and Claudia mingled among other guests. A brief meeting had taken place earlier that afternoon, at which each member of the team was assigned a post.

The four course dinner was served by caterers, some of whom were undercover officers. Count Safini gave a heartfelt speech in his mother's honor. More speeches and anecdotes of the celebrated woman's long life followed, some of which were quite hilarious.

Isabella drummed her fingers on the seat of the taxi—a sign of her growing impatience. The drive to the villa would have taken half an hour if it had not been for the evening traffic, and then a punctured rear tire. "I'm not that heavy," she mumbled to herself, frustrated by the additional delay.

The car stopped at the gate leading into the long drive up to the villa. The young guard peered inside the cabin, and satisfied by the formal dress, concluded that its passenger was a tardy guest. He waved them through the gate onto the large estate. Then there was a loud bang. The taxi swerved, coming to a stop in a small ditch.

"So sorry, *signora*," the driver said, opening the cab door. "Another flat tire," he explained, apologetic and embarrassed. Isabella was fuming. She opened her purse and threw the fare onto the driver's seat, deciding to walk the rest of the way. The driver called after her, but ignoring him, she continued marching up to the residence. She could hear the sound of music as she drew closer, which tamed her frustration and allowed her to calm her breathing.

Chapter Fifty-Nine

After dinner, Peter and Lana joined the guests in the ballroom, which was filled with classical music played by a small orchestra. The foxtrot and waltz were Lana's favorites, although she was also partial to the tango.

Isabella composed herself prior to climbing the steps up to the main entrance. Here she was stopped by Santo. From the stairs, Patrizio recognized her.

"Sir James, we have a visitor at the door," he said quietly into his microphone, slowly moving toward her.

"I'm coming," Grant replied, walking out of the ballroom and leaving 'Lady Claudia' in the middle of a waltz. Not to draw attention, she gallantly went to get another flute of champagne from the bar.

"It's OK, Santo," Grant said, taking the uninvited guest by the arm and escorting her behind the winding staircase.

"What are you doing here?" he demanded. "Are you crazy?"

"Where is he?" she asked, looking around. An elderly couple walked past. Grant and Isabella smiled politely, before continuing their heated but hushed discussion.

"You were supposed to stay put!"

"Don't tell me what to do. I mean business. This man must be caught tonight. Not tomorrow or next week, but tonight!" she said adamantly without breaking eye contact.

"We've got it under control," Grant affirmed. "You'll get your man tonight."

Isabella wasn't convinced. She walked out from behind the stairs and toward the bar. Here she was met by Claudia, who ordered her a diet Coke, which she gracefully accepted.

"You are a naughty girl," Claudia whispered.

"I can see him. Who is that blond bimbo?" Isabella asked. Before her question could be answered, two middle-aged gentlemen, approached inviting them to dance. Isabella loved to waltz. It was something her father had taught her before her wedding to Nick. Her dance partner was gallant, and for a brief moment she forgot about Peter Steil. The music stopped briefly before the next song. Isabella thanked the man, excusing herself to observe Peter from the bar. Grant approached her.

"Do you have all exits covered?" she asked without looking at him.

"Yes, of course. Why?" he asked while ordering a drink.

A reply didn't come. He turned to see Isabella walk up to Peter, who had finished dancing with the young blond. Instinctively, he spoke into his microphone, alerting all units to be in position. He was horrified at what he saw next.

"Care to tango?" Isabella asked a surprised Peter. He obliged, feeling that he didn't have much choice.

"You don't recognize me, do you?" she asked, smiling. They danced, both with a forced smile plastered on their faces. Then it dawned on him. Peter had many faults, but he had an outstanding memory for faces and voices. Despite the time that had passed he knew who she was.

"We met in LA almost eighteen months ago," he said smugly, looking for a reaction. "And you threw up in my helicopter last week."

"Yes, I did," she confirmed. "You are right all the way. How's Patrick?" Isabella taunted. Suddenly his smile vanished. "How are your parents? You know, the ones that you killed," she said more menacingly.

There were agents all around the villa covering every exit. Through their earpieces they listened.

Peter suddenly recalled that the lovely lady he had met in LA months ago had been introduced by their mutual friend as a detective of the LAPD. Now she was standing here and he knew why. There was no going back. The adrenaline built in his body, priming him for escape.

Peter stopped dancing and extracted himself from her grip. The tension between Isabella and her man were running high. The other guests were for now oblivious to this masquerade of friendly dancing and the hostility it hid.

At that moment, Lana returned from the bathroom to find her lover in the company of another woman. Fueled by jealousy, she charged toward Isabella and pushed her aside, positioning herself in front of Peter. He looked past her at the nearest exit: the French doors leading out to the terrace.

"Darling, what's going on here?" Lana asked, confused by the change in his mood.

Peter shoved her aside without answering and charged toward the nearest exit.

"All units go!" Grant commanded. "Subject on the run!"

Isabella lunged at Peter, who threw her against the wall. She cried out in agony. Grant tackled him, crashing onto the harp player of the small orchestra. Peter punched Grant hard, splitting open his lip. The other officers tried to block Peter's path, but failed. The fugitive was fit and quick. As he dodged the officers, Peter pulled out his gun and opened fire.

To the sounds of women screaming, Santo gave chase. He threw himself at Peter, catching him before he could reach the door leading onto the terrace. He dragged him back by his coat tails and pushed him against a table, knocking vases over and gifts onto the floor.

Peter lost his grip on gun. He wasn't worried. He had a spare latched to his ankle, and he had been well-trained for combat. To him, this fight was no different to past wars he had fought in. Peter pushed a waiter holding a silver tray of crystal glasses out of his way, sending him crashing to the ground, and made for the terrace. The noise of shattering glass and silver ware was deafening.

Most of the guests were in shock, not knowing what to make of the scene that had unfolded. Confused and too frightened to move, they stood as far as they could out of harm's way.

Count Safini wheeled his elderly mother into another room despite her protests.

"I was enjoying that. Was that part of the surprise?" she asked. He didn't answer, knowing that with the onset of dementia earlier that year, she would have trouble understanding.

During the commotion, Claudia had removed her gown, under which she wore leggings and a tank top. Kicking off her shoes, she followed Peter onto the terrace, chasing him as he ran toward the garage where he would have a selection of fast cars to get away in. He opened fire at her, hitting her in the arm. She slowed but kept running. Patrizio came from behind, chasing their man into the large garage. The two men fought on the hood of the car, sliding onto the ground. Peter managed to free himself and temporarily blinded Patrizio by throwing gravel into his face.

The fugitive got into the Alfa Spider, found the keys in the glove compartment, turned on the ignition and revved the engine. Patrizio had by this time quickly composed and repositioned himself behind the car, obstructing the exit. Peter didn't care and placed the gear in reverse. Patrizio jumped out of the way of the reversing car, but Claudia jumped onto its hood. Peter swerved, trying to shake her off. She hung on with her good arm while pointing her gun at him through the windshield.

"Stop, you bastard!" she said before firing. The glass cracked, but she'd missed his head by inches. The car slowed, running off the path crashing into a fence.

"Get out of the car!" Isabella ordered once she'd reached him. Her lower back and right hip ached from the fall. Ignoring the discomfort in her lower abdomen, she held her ground.

Claudia slid off the bonnet and threw the door open forcefully. Peter didn't move, but just sat with his weapon aimed at her.

"Who should I shoot first, you or your little friend?" he mocked, wiping blood off a cut on his check.

Isabella could shoot to kill or wound from the position she was standing. The other agents neared but kept a distance, as they had planned in the tactical briefing.

"Who do you want to shoot first?" Claudia asked, initially catching him off guard. Peter regained his arrogant composure and tauntingly blew her a kiss.

Isabella had had enough of this cat and mouse game. Her hand was steady. She aimed and pulled the trigger.

Chapter Sixty

Los Angeles, two months later

The Peter Steil trial had not been a long, drawn out one. The jury was in the process of final deliberations, and today would return their verdict.

Special Agent Claudia Conti sat in the sparse courtroom along with a few members of the public, including Lilly Sands and her sister. The prosecution and defense had taken their seats and waited patiently.

Claudia had been impressed by Isabella's tenacity throughout the investigation.

"Hey," she whispered as she saw Isabella enter the room, motioning Isabella to sit next to her.

"How was the ultrasound?" she asked, still whispering.

"All good," Isabella answered, smiling.

The bailiff entered with Peter from a side door and positioned Peter next to his lawyer. He was dressed in a dark suit, his expression impassive. Next, the judge returned from his chambers and took his place at the bench. A second side door opened, allowing each of the twelve jurors to return to their seats. Silence.

The judge spoke. "Have you reached a verdict?"

A man in his forties stood and spoke, addressing the judge and courtroom.

"We have, your Honor."

"How do you find the defendant?" the judge asked, without much inflection in his tone.

"We, the jury, find the defendant, Peter Adam Steil, guilty on all counts of murder in the first degree."

There was a sigh of relief from all in attendance. The accused remained expressionless as he was led from the courtroom back to the jailhouse. Isabella and Claudia hugged, then shook hands with the Sands family.

Peter had given nothing away concerning the matter of the disappearance of the real Peter Claasen. It was his way of maintaining some control over those who had hunted and found him. But the investigation had been reopened, resulting in a collaborative approach between the Dutch and Mexican authorities.

Nick and Grant waited on the steps of the courthouse for Isabella and Claudia to emerge. It was obvious from their expressions that justice had been served.

"Well, I think this is cause for a celebration," Nick announced, taking his wife by the hand.

"I couldn't agree more," both women said in unison. Grant smiled warmly at Claudia, who returned the gesture. The foursome walked together to a local Italian place where they spent most of the afternoon discussing everything but work.

It had been a long, arduous journey. Now it was time for Isabella to relax and focus on a new beginning.

Epilogue

One year later

Isabella returned to a more peaceful mindset after Peter Steil's conviction and two consecutive life sentences. She gave birth to a healthy baby girl, Maria, named after her own mother, who both she and Nick doted on. A very happy time indeed.

Grant and Claudia became friends and eventually started dating, which surprised some given their mutual love of independence. They both joined meditation and yoga classes, which helped tame their fiery spirits.

Countess Lana Safini gave birth to twin boys. Her parents were not happy about their daughter having children out of wedlock, but came to adore the 'little angels'.

Detective Mann decided to retire from the force after the Steil and Mason cases concluded. He had realized that police work no longer suited him and opted for a more peaceful existence. His passion was skiing, and he became a skiing instructor.

Lilly Sands, Mason's widow, laid her late husband's body to rest in a small cemetery not far from her home.

The offer to partake in an episode of *America's Most Wanted* presented itself. Lilly declined.

Santo and Patrizio were promoted to join Special Forces of the Italian police, after their outstanding contribution to the case. They were thrilled.

Peter Steil would in time become a distant memory to most, but to some he would never be forgotten.

Printed in Australia
AUHW010737100719
314451AU00005B/10